Jax's Vengeance

Editing by William Burkhart at SIXDOOM LITERARY LLC.

OTHER TITLES BY
RAVEN LEITHE HARLOW

THE SILVERTHORNE PRINCES
CASSIDY'S WAR (PART ONE)

THE DIVINE SAGA
INITIUM (BOOK ONE)
DIABOLUS (BOOK TWO) *Coming Soon 2025*

STAND-ALONE NOVELS
SANDCASTLES IN RHODES

To my amazing husband and children, your faith in me has been the pillar of my confidence, my biggest supporters without whom none of this would have been possible.

To my cherished friends and family, your unwavering support has been invaluable on this remarkable journey.

To my avid readers and fans, this one will take you down a rabbit hole; tugging on your heartstrings and toying with your emotions. You may want to bring a flashlight as you delve through these dark and twisted pages.

To those who do not like to read the trigger warnings in books, I suggest you skip the next two pages.

TRIGGER WARNING

Some readers may find the following list of themes depicted in this book to be offensive and disturbing. Therefore, please proceed with caution and prioritize your mental well-being. If you find any of these topics distressing, you may want to skip this content or ensure you have support available.

Explicit and graphic sexual content
Strong/Explicit Language
LGTBQ+ relationships
Adultery
Multiple partners
Betrayal
Blood Play
Blade Play
Bondage/Restrained
Dubious consent
Revenge
Arson / Fire
Violence
Torture
Blood and gore
Battle scenes
Murder
Sacrificial deaths
Infanticide
Suicidal thoughts and actions
Necromancy

JAX'S VENGEANCE

Betrayal

Grief and mourning

Depression

Anxiety

Drowning

Stalking

Voyeurism

Suffocation

Mutilation / dismemberment

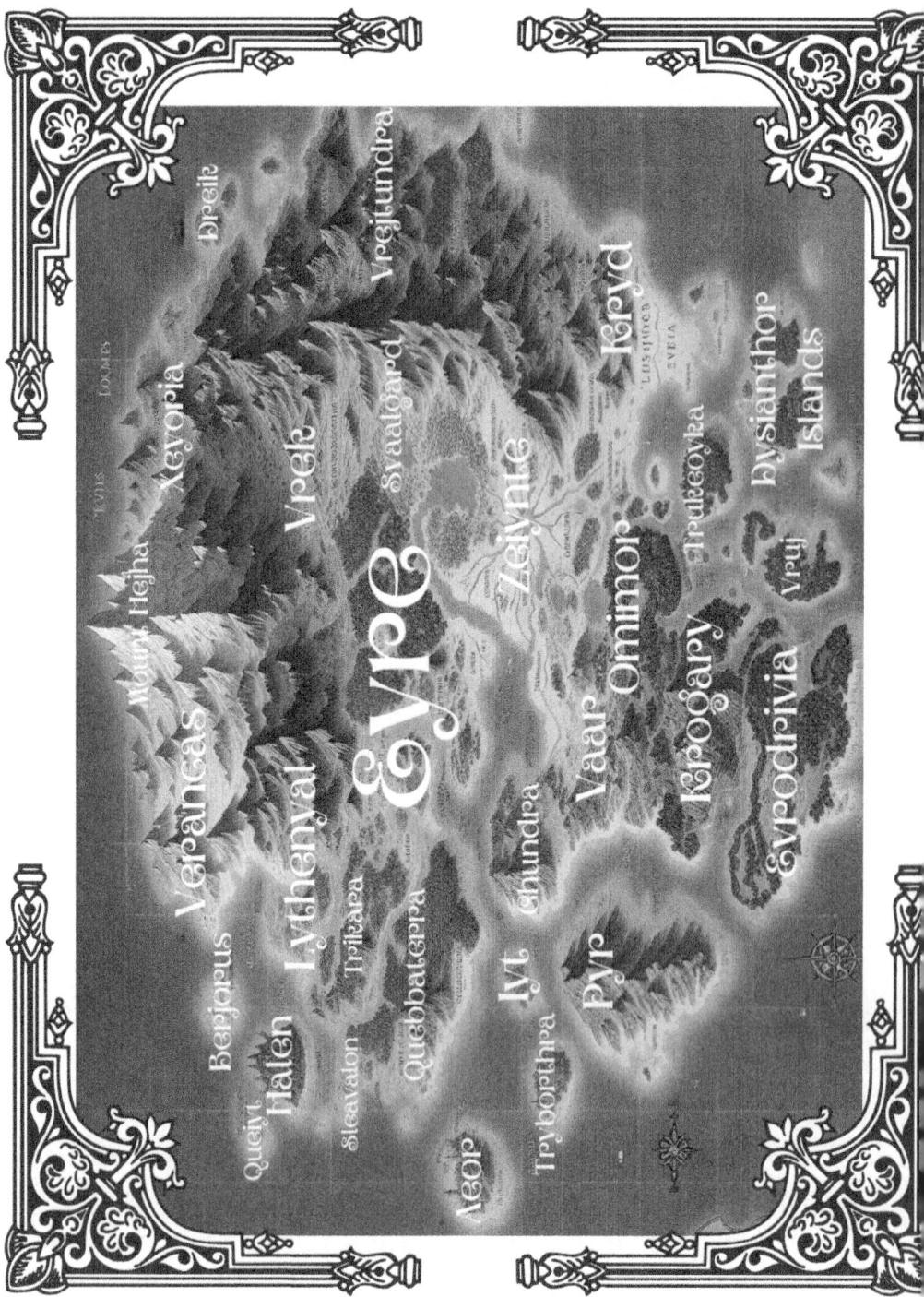

Jax's Vengeance is the second part of 'The Silverthorne Princes' duology. The story unfolds in the fantastical world of Xeyiera, primarily within Eyre, the largest kingdom. Given the many references to various kingdoms, I have created the accompanying map to illustrate the geographic allocations of each realm; from the rugged mountain ranges and serene beaches, to the barren deserts and lush swamps of Xeyiera.

Below are some of the pronunciations for the names of places or people mentioned in this book:

Xeyiera = [ex-year-ah]
Eyre = [ay-yer]
Estoria = [est-or-ee-ah]
Hehja = [hay-yah]
Svaalgard = [svahl-gar-d]
Borjus = [boar-jiss]
Lythenyal = [life-en-yal]
Halen = [hay-len]
Alyiah = [al-lee-yah]
Torvus = [tour-vuh-ss]

"Here I opened wide the door;
Darkness there, and nothing more."
- Edgar Allan Poe, The Raven

PROLOGUE

PRESENT DAY

Cassidy

Screams of terror infiltrated the castle. The clatter of metal armor thundered through the corridor. Guards flocked to their designated stations. The sounds of chaos echoed against the stone walls.

A stampede of feet stormed through the halls of the castle, defying the security of the safest place in Estoria. This castle was the most fortified building in the whole of Eyre. Nothing should have been able to penetrate its borders.

Worry consumed the King, my soulmate, these past few years. Ever since our only son was born, Logan has been beside himself with fear; afraid everything he has achieved will be taken from him. The words from a seer only intensified the matter. *"Evil waits for its moment to strike, leaving only death in its wake."*

Despite all Logan's meticulous planning, the upgrades to the castle's defenses, and more guards appointed, this evil had still slipped through the cracks; infiltrating the castle, plundering its serenity with one singular motive - to destroy.

I heard it climbing the grand staircase with ease. I felt its harrowing and malicious intent while stalking the corridors. I watched through its eyes, stopping outside the heavy oak door of my room. My stomach churned at the distinct odor of blood dripping from the heart clutched in its fingertips.

Haunted by the words of the Elders, a shiver ran down my spine. *"One day you will live to regret the decision you made."*

That day has come.

ONE

Jax

A high-pitched, ear-splitting cry ripped through my skull, shattering any notion of sleep. Relentless wails, taking little time to catch its breath between each one. They reverberated in my skull and sent shivers along my spine. Cries of an infant new to the world, disoriented and scared, having left the safety and comfort of its mother's womb. This was not any baby, it was another obstruction in my path. Another obstacle to overcome before taking what should be mine - the throne, the kingdom. *Cassidy.*

Squeezing my eyes shut, I tried not to picture her, but she was forever etched into my mind. Her tousled brunette curls, moss-green eyes twinkling with satisfaction. Those plump pink lips curled in a satisfied grin. She was always the most beautiful in the aftermath of her orgasm. It had been over a year since I had last seen her face.

A sharp pain sliced through my chest as I recalled our last encounter. The clash of metal against metal as swords collided and armor destroyed. Chaos encapsulated us. Yet as I held her, staring into those eyes, my heart was breaking. She had made her choice.

My eyes snapped open; the sudden brightness assaulted my eyes. Instead of the grimy stone walls I had been expecting to see, sterile white walls surrounded me. Clean and crisp, harsh white lights above, illuminating the scene. In my arms was the baby, swaddled in a pastel blue blanket with gold embroidered initials FS. There was a murmur of voices to the side of me, but my eyes fixed on the child, tears blurring my vision.

"Welcome to the world, Prince Felix." My gaze darted from the babe to the owner of the voice. His velvet tones sounded like music to my ears. My heart stopped. I was an intruder, watching through the eyes of my soulmate. I felt the sudden warmth of happiness flood through her body as she stared into my brother's eyes. Cassidy's contentment stung more than grit in an open wound.

I watched as he grazed the side of her cheek. The cool brush of metal against her skin tingles on my own. My anger simmered at the sight of him and at the child that now lay sleeping in her arms. *They have sealed my fate and their own.*

Delicate, feather-like fingers rested on my shoulder. Warm breath fluttered along my nape where her lips lingered. "Jax?" A woman's voice murmured, pulling me back to my body. "Another bad dream?" My head twisted to the sound of her voice, her face so close our noses touched. My vision slowly come back to focus, seeing her dark brown eyes staring into my own looking glassy with exhaustion.

The woman beside me with flawless tanned skin and thick dark lips served as a stark reminder. As gorgeous as she was; she was not who I wanted her to be. Alyiah could never fill the Cassidy-shaped void in my life. No matter how many weeks, months or even years pass, the dull ache in my heart never ceases.

Alyiah's lips fluttered against mine, her hand creeping its way to my groin. "Let me take your mind off it," she purred, her hand slipping beneath the sheets. She leaned closer. The scent of our sex from earlier lingered on her skin, like a hypnotic and alluring perfume, making my cock hard in her hand.

I nodded, succumbing to my need to feel something, *anything*, other than the pain that gnawed at my insides. *I will take back what is mine.* I allowed Alyiah to dominate for once. Letting her push me back down against the bed sheets as she mounted my cock like a jockey. Her heat welcomed my full length, coaxing a moan from her parted lips as she ground her hips against mine; increasing her rhythm as she called my name over and over. She grabbed her bouncing breasts, pinching her hard nipples.

My moans were automatic and instinctive in contrast to her genuine pleasure. The swell of my balls was natural and animalistic, derived from Alyiah's movements. I wasn't *feeling* the moment like Alyiah. This was nothing more than a distraction. Despite Alyiah's best efforts, snippets of Cassidy's face flashed through my mind. I could still feel the fierce love for the child that should never have been born. The sensation of her unabashed happiness in the arms of my brother made my anger prickle.

I gritted my teeth and snarled, throwing Alyiah backwards. My hands pinning her wrists to the bed, *I have to be in control.* My teeth sunk into the side of her neck, not deep enough to draw blood, but hard enough to make her squeal in shock. Violent red teeth marks left on her tanned flesh.

My shaft thrust into her hard; deep and unrelenting as my fury became my driving force. The happier Cassidy felt; the more violent I became. My fingers wrapped around Alyiah's throat, blocking her windpipe, suffocating her slowly.

Alyiah's eyes popped open in surprise; her nails clawed at my skin as she tried to speak. "Jax..." her raspy voice croaked. "I... can't...br-" Scowling down at her, I removed my hand. I smirked as she gasped in relief, her chest rising as she took several deep breaths. I could tell from her facial expression I had scared her. Still, I continued to fuck her hard. I clutched a fist full of her dark locks and pulled.

Within moments, she was writhing beneath me. Her hips bucking against mine to match my brutal pace, but I could not let go of the thoughts of Cassidy. No matter how hard I tried to push her aside, memories of taking Cassidy would prevail. I recalled the sensation of sinking my cock deep into her. Reliving the pleasure of hearing my name roll off her tongue. It was the only way to take me over the edge.

I was never truly satisfied unless I was thinking of her. Pretending it was her soft skin beneath mine, not Alyiah's. Wishing it was Cassidy purring my name. My mind sought comparisons between the two of them, even though I knew they were total opposites. Alyiah knew what she liked, striving for her own lustful gain. Whereas Cassidy was new to it all - unaccustomed to her sexual desires and open to her curious fantasies.

The flushed crimson in her cheeks when she discovered something that aroused her was an allure to me. I wanted to give her everything her heart desired. I wanted to please her every need - even if that meant including others. That was the main reason I kept Alyiah around. Our tryst with Cassidy, the pleasure we both made her feel, was the only connection I felt.

I yanked on the hair in my hands, pulling out before my seed exploded in Alyiah's warmth. Instead, it spewed over her stomach while I chided myself. *Cassidy is the only woman I want to plant my seed inside.*

"I love you Jax," Alyiah sighed, her fingertips tracing the side of my face. My eyes scanned her face, seeing the softness in her eyes and the glazed look from her climax. As I stared down my nose at her, I felt nothing more than pity. I was only using her for my selfish gain - to take as much from her as possible until I regained my rightful place in Eyre.

One thing was crystal clear; she would *never* replace Cassidy. I bit my tongue, holding back my response. *I will never love you.*

TWO

Anger, like a blazing fire, surged through my veins. Blinding me from everything around me as I scarpered like a coward away from the battlefield. Flanking me were the bedraggled remnants of my men.

It was devastating, *infuriating*, to see the full extent of my humiliating defeat. Lifeless Trolls littered the path as I fled. Forms that had once invoked fear were now nothing more than food for the worms. Each corpse was a stark reminder of the fierce, loyal men my brother had on his side. Beneath my feet, the once green terrain was crimson. Traipsing through the thick and sticky sludge as their blood began to dry.

With each step I forced myself to take, I felt the bond tug: trying to pull me back, refusing to leave my soulmate behind me. Yet the pain of her choice forced me to keep putting one foot in front of the other. No matter how far the distance expanded between us, the bond would never break. I didn't want to leave her, but my dented pride propelled me forward.

Had I stood my ground, finished what I had started, the war would be over. My brother would be dead and I would not be exiled. I would have had everything that my heart desired - the throne, the kingdom, and *her*.

My stomach wrenched and my chest tore apart inside as I neared the bordering trees. Once I went beyond them, everything I wanted would be left behind. Everything I had been fighting for. It was also where the lifeless form of my sister lay contorted and trampled, only several feet from me. She was like a double-edged blade; her vindictive and manipulative ways had led to her demise. Demi's desire to kill Cassidy was only brought to my attention after it was too late. I would never have let it happen, had I known sooner. Her twisted love for me, deeper than what a sibling should feel, had corrupted her soul.

For a moment, I stopped, conflicted by my feelings towards her. *Had she not involved the trolls, this war may not have happened. I would have had more time to convince Cassidy that I was the one her heart desired. I could be the prince who would make the better King.* Yet I could not leave her body here. I would not allow my twin's corpse to rot in an unmarked grave, eaten by animals, or worse.

I scooped her up into my arms as my tears blinded me. This magnificent, powerful and demanding woman lay like a broken doll in my arms. Her translucent hair tumbled over my arm, now streaked with scarlet. It was jarring to look at the vibrancy of her blood against her porcelain complexion. A look of pain, of remorse even, forever etched into her facial features.

"Sire, let me take her." Hands were pulling at her body, trying to take it away from me. I snarled; my eyes snapping up to look at the owner of the voice. Torvus, my second in command. A brute of a man, all muscle and tattoos with a heavy black beard braided to his chest. A true warrior who had shown nothing but loyalty to my cause.

My anger simmered beneath my skin as I let him take her from my arms. "We will give her a good burial." He said, his eyes raking over her face. There was a sadness that had washed over him. No longer this fierce brute who wielded a double-bladed ax, but a sorrowful shell of a man who had lost his lover. *A lover I never knew she had.* I watched as he cradled her limp body, clutching it to his chest. In life, she must have meant something to him. Though I doubted he knew the truth - that those feelings were not reciprocated.

His eyes flashed up at mine, hard and cold. "What is the plan, Sire?" he asked through gritted teeth. "What is our next move?"

I remained silent, the pull to Cassidy still tearing at my insides. My anger at her decision to choose Logan over me had glued my mouth shut. In truth, I had never expected defeat; or at least to live after it. I had believed that I would have been the victor. That I would have watched the sunrise the following morning, sat on the throne with Cassidy by my side.

The battlefield was now quiet. I stole one last look over my shoulder as it disappeared behind the thick trunks of the evergreens. I could no longer see Cassidy or the events that unfolded, but I could see through hers. the Elders surrounded them both, looking down upon them. Logan was too weak to open his eyes, his dismembered hand still discarded on the ground. I felt tears rolling down her cheeks, her chest heaving as she pleaded for their help. *"Please save him. I love him... I chose him."*

A stab of pain sliced through my chest, doubling over and gritting my teeth.

"Prince... sire! Are you ok?" Another of my men asked, rushing to my side. His powerful hands hoisted me upright. "Are you hurt?"

I shook my head, allowing him to support my weight. The anger within me scorched my insides and rendered me breathless and shaking. *This is not over.*

What am I meant to do now? I had no plan. *This is not meant to be my destiny.* As we trudged forwards across kingdom borders, I tried to concoct a plan of our exile, but the consistent thrum of Cassidy's feelings was a hindrance I could not ignore. Snippets of her vision blurred my own; watching Logan's body on a hospital bed; healers surrounding him. Every time she caught sight of the stump where his right hand should be, I felt her anger.

I wanted to hate her, to wish them both dead. I wanted this bond between the three of us destroyed. *But how can I hate the person who saved my life? How could I loathe whom I am pre-destined to love?*

With every step I took, the gap between us increased and I prayed our bond would fade. Hoping that I would not have to live a lifetime of torture. That I would not feel her every emotion and see through her eyes day after day until my last. *Has Cassidy saved my life or set me up for a life of misery?*

Yet, there was a flicker of hope that lived within me. There was a reason she had not chosen Logan straight away when faced with the ultimatum. A reason she had allowed me to escape. *She loves me too.*

No matter how small this glimmer of hope was, I clung to it. It was all I had left. Aside from my memories of the short time spent in her company. The way her eyes lit up when she smiled. The soft touch of her skin against mine. The melodic purr of her voice when she spoke. A knot formed in my stomach; *would she have chosen me if I had been wounded instead of Logan?*

"Sire... where will we go from here?" Torvus' voice snapped me back to the present, his arms still cradling the corpse of my twin sister. Another stab to the heart. My thoughts clouded as my eyes raked over her lifeless form. A plan formed as I stared at her. *One that will tarnish my soul.*

The road ahead forked. A wooden sign showed two arrows. One marked the path to the right leading to Verancas. The other on the left would take us to Lythenyal. My chest clenched. The last time I had been to Verancas had been with Cassidy. Our tryst with Alyiah and her girlfriend Eleanor, a special moment I could never forget. It had unlocked the curious and adventurous side within Cassidy; a side I wanted to see more of. I wanted to spend our lives satisfying her every desire. Traveling and fucking, marking every corner of this world with our love.

Lythenyal was the city on the brink of the ocean. Home to the only port in Xeyiera that could offer direct routes to the islands of Halen and Berjorus: the two kingdoms most difficult to reach from Eyre. I made a mental note to research them both before landing on their shores. *They may be the perfect kingdoms to lie low for a while.*

"Right," I barked, my eyes still fixated on the sign. "I have business in Verancas..." I let my words trail off as my eyes darted back to my sister in Torvus' arms. He nodded, as if he understood, but he thought wrong if he believed this would be the ultimate resting place of my sister.

I pressed forward, leading the battle-wounded men along the rocky, single-track road. The foot of Mount Hejha appeared before us, reminding me of Cassidy. Recalling the sparkle of awe in her eyes she looked up at the largest mountain in all of Xeyiera. It towered above the clouds - ominous and intimidating. I could still see her now, standing there wondering if the legends were true. Whether the peak of the mountains was the entrance to Heaven and beneath our very feet was the gate to Hell.

I swallowed the lump that had formed in the back of my throat. *This right here, facing a life without Cassidy, is Hell.* The men slowed behind me, the crunch of the dusty gravel beneath their feet quietened. "Sire?" one of them asked. His voice was unsure as his eyes followed my gaze up to the highest visible point of the mountain. "Are we-?"

I shook my head, turning to give him a small smile. "What is your name again?"

"Nathaniel, sire, but most just call me Nate."

I nodded, taking in his scrawny frame and boyish features. Clean shaven, long mud-brown hair tied back with leather straps. He could not be any older than seventeen. "How did you end up in the battle, Nate? You don't look old enough to be a soldier."

His facial features hardened, his jaw set, and his fists clenched at his sides. "I *chose* to fight alongside you, Prince Jax. The trolls took my family; my parents, my kid-sister. Prince Logan done nothing! He stood by and allowed it to happen and when he and the Elders stepped in... it was already too late."

Guilt tried to creep over me, knowing the trolls had been my sister's idiotic plan, but I pushed it down deep. Burying it in the depths of my consciousness. *There is nothing I can do to change it now.* "Thank you, Nate, for your loyalty." I nodded. "And I am sorry for your loss."

Nate gave a small nod before clearing his throat, "and I am sorry about yours too... you would have made a great King."

Anger ignited within, clutching at his collar and lifting him into the air. Determination simmered beneath the surface, spurring my feet back into action. "I still *will*... Our fight will not have been in vain... I *will* take back what should be mine."

The other men cheered behind me. All but Torvus. He remained intensively concentrated on Demi's corpse in his arms.

"All hail *King* Jax." they roared, evoking a small smirk across my face. *I can get used to that.*

THREE

I was close, *so fucking close.* My whole body was buzzing; alive with electricity as Eleanor's tongue lapped at my heat. I was weak. My nerves went into overdrive after her persistent teasing. But she was ready to let me cum. Refusing to break eye contact as she buried her head between my thighs.

With one hand, she thrust a black plastic shaft deep into my slit while the other worked a much thicker one into her own. Her tongue performed acrobatics over my clit. I was on the brink of orgasm, my hands clutching at her hair, holding her head in place as my body buckled beneath her.

"Eleanor…" I gasped, unable to hold back my wave of pleasure any longer. "Fuck…don't stop."

There was a movement to the left; a shadow that caught my attention from my peripheral vision. I tried to hold it in, noticing he was not alone, but it was too late. My orgasm crashed through me. My core gripping the phallic toy as my inner walls convulsed around it, leaving me breathless.

"Jax?" I panted, sitting upright on my lounge floor as Eleanor pulled out the toy. My nectar dribbled down her chin as she wiped at her satisfied grin. All eyes were on me, not only his. Five others stood beside him, all waiting for me to climax before interrupting. Jax was the closest, a prominent bulge in his pants. *He always liked to watch, and was never afraid to show his arousal.* The others looked more sheepish, at least trying to cover their erections. It would have made for quite a party. Apart from one man standing behind Jax, disinterested in me. Once the haze of my climatic high dispersed, I realized he was holding a bloodied corpse in his arms.

"What the fuck?" I yelled, scrambling backwards on the floor. I tried to distance myself from the woman laying limp and broken only a few feet away. My eyes scanned them all, taking in the dented and damaged armor they wore. Eyeing up the relatively fresh wounds on their bodies. Their faces were decorated with dried blood splatter. *Fresh from the battle.*

"Alyiah… I need your help," Jax mumbled. I shook my head instinctively, my hut suddenly feeling too hot and too cramped with so many bodies inside. I glared at Jax before my eyes swept over the body of the woman. I did not recognize her; it was not who I thought it was. *Cassidy.*

"Jax… what is going on?" I asked, throwing on my clothes and getting to my feet, noticing Eleanor doing the same. She glowered at them, unable to hide her anger at Jax's intrusion when it was her turn next to be on the receiving end. She gathered up the toys, dumping them in the nearby wooden crate.

"Al, come find me when they are gone," Eleanor said, brushing past them all. "I want no part of whatever *this* is." She stormed out, not giving me a backwards glance.

I watched her leave in silence; she knew I was a fool when it came to Jax, that I held a soft spot for him since we first met many years ago. Although she would never admit it, Eleanor did not like being second best to him. She did not take kindly to the fact that Jax would always hold a special place in my heart and between my legs.

Our eyes connected, and for a few moments I could feel his pain; the rage in his eyes like hot coals. He had the look of a tortured animal; the haunting look of despair forever etched into my memory. A flicker of hope and a momentary burst of happiness thrummed in my chest. *Cassidy did not choose him.*

Jax winced as he took the woman's corpse from the man before placing it on my couch. Wincing in pain, trying not to lean to one side. His thigh was bandaged, with only strips of fabric torn from his shirt. He was the only one who was not still adorned in damaged armor. His muscular torso peeked through the rips of his shirt, revealing more bruises and cuts. It was clear the battle had not ended well. *He is lucky to be alive.*

"I couldn't leave her there." Jax murmured as he backed away from her. His gaze caught mine, noticing my quizzical look. "This is, *was*, my twin sister, Demi… she- she, um, got caught up in the battle." His voice cracked as he struggled to explain.

The men who were still standing near the door looked at one another, unsure of their leader's motives. But I knew what he wanted. *I always do.*

"Alyiah... she was all I had left..." I rushed to him, feeling him crumple the moment I wrapped my arms around him. I had never seen Jax without a sexy smirk curled on his lips. Whenever he came to visit he was always confident and unburdened by his emotions, aside from his lust. It was what I enjoyed most about his visits. *He always left satisfied, too.* It was unsettling to feel his sobs rattle through my body as I held him.

"I need you to help me find him." Jax mumbled, his mouth buried in the crook of my neck.

"No... oh no... Jax, *that* is a terrible idea." I said, pulling away to look at him, noticing his eyes fixed on the lifeless body of his sister.

A fire danced through his eyes; his hand clasped around my throat. "You *will* help me Alyiah..." Jax hissed with a voice as cold as steel. His fingers tightened, blocking my windpipe.

"I demand you take me to him, the necromancer... the Phantom."

I shook my head, gasping. "Nothing good ever comes from-" His grasp squeezed harder, cutting off the rest of my sentence. I could feel my eyes popping out of their sockets. My mascara ran as tears escaped them. My lungs were deprived of oxygen, my muscles weak and pathetic as I tried to claw at his hand frantically. Jax did not move a muscle. His eyes penetrated mine as if I was the only person in the room.

"He is your *father,* after all."

I had no time to prepare myself for his sudden release, collapsing in a heap on the floor at his feet. I gasped for air, rubbing the sore spots where his nails had dug into the flesh on my neck as I stared at him, dumbstruck. "Jax... you can't be *serious*?"

I cowered under his glare as he stood over me wearing a menacing grin. "Oh, I *am* serious, Alyiah..." he paused, his fingertips curling under my chin. Lifting my face to look directly into his eyes once more.

"Now, are you going to do this the *easy* way..." his hands slid down to my throat once more. I felt a strength in his chokehold I had never experienced from him before. The stench of dried blood emanated from his skin, clotting in my throat as his grip tightened. "Or are you going to make me do this the *hard* way?"

FOUR

Logan

Everything I could ever want or need, I held in my arms. The most important and precious gifts the Gods had ever granted me - my wife Cassidy, and my son Felix. Enveloped in my arms, the pair of them slept. Blissfully unaware of the terror that permeated my thoughts. My fear of not being able to protect them. *Jax is still out there...*

A shiver ran down my spine as flashbacks of the battlefield played out in my mind. Intense pain consumed me as blood poured from my missing right hand. The sensation of the hot, sticky rivulets cascading down my arm and staining the ground at my feet. A white-hot fire radiated from my wrist. Every beat of my heart pumped more of my life force out of my wound.

I remembered hitting the ground like a ton of bricks and the sudden feeling of paralysis numbing every inch of my body. I had lost too much blood - I was dying. I was nothing more than a weak, pathetic loser. *Cassidy deserves better than either of us.*

My mind reeled; I was stunned I'd die by my brother's hand. *I'd hoped things wouldn't reach this point.* I was angry at myself for being too loyal, too sentimental to deliver a fatal blow to Jax. *Now I have lost the one thing that was worth fighting for. The one thing that I wanted above the throne and the kingdom.*

"Logan?" The sound of her voice stirred me from my reverie, my eyes drawn to hers. "Logan, you're trembling... what's wrong?"

I looked at my solid iron hand; the substitute crafted for me in the battle's aftermath. Cassidy's father was the most prestigious blacksmith in Eyre. My coat of arms and intricate designs adorned the back of my hand. The palm was sleek and smooth. Attached with a thick metal cuff to hide the grotesque stump. It was cumbersome and heavy. Awkward and always cold to the touch.

Cassidy avoided looking at it. Even now, she blamed herself for my dismemberment. I suffered because she had not chosen sooner, before it had escalated. Witnessing her sadness, I felt a powerful urge to console her. To prove to her that losing a limb was a small sacrifice. *Cassidy chose me and that is all that matters.*

Her battlefield voice made me smile, though I'd told her to stay safe by the lake. Low and distant, her words muffled, but she was there. Her hands wrapped fabric around my wound to staunch the blood flow.

"I have made my choice... please help him!" I had no strength at the time to open my eyes, even as her arms cradled my body and her tears rained down on me. I knew I had to live - to endure and persevere. I would spend my entire life proving to Cassidy I was worthy of her love. I never wanted her to doubt her decision.

"I will never regret choosing you, Logan," Cassidy said through our telepathic link as she snuggled into me. My arms instinctively tightened around her, feeling our baby stir in her arms. His sudden cry pierced the silence of the night, tugging at my heartstrings.

"Everything is perfect." I buried my head in her hair, kissing the top of her head to disguise my trembling lips. "I love you, Cassidy... I will never stop loving you."

The child continued to wail for a few moments, its face crumpled and its arms flailing at its side. I felt helpless. More scared of being responsible for the safety of the next King than I had when facing my impending death.

"Logan, you will be an amazing father..." She revealed a breast, full and heavy, for him to suckle on. I watched in awe as she acted instinctively and naturally. Nurturing our son, seeming to know what he needed without being told.

"You are a fantastic king... a perfect role model for Felix..." Cassidy tilted her head to look at me, her lips seeking mine. "I will forever stand by my decision, Logan... I just wish I had made it sooner."

The moment our lips touched; I felt the rush of her love. Our connection strengthened as a surge of electricity passed between us. It filled me with courage. Sparked a determination within me to be everything she needed. I would give them both everything they deserved. A life of unyielding happiness and unconditional love.

Yet, a nagging doubt persisted; Jax was still alive because Cassidy had let him escape. The bond still tied her to him until one of them took their last breath. I knew my brother would never accept his defeat. Jax would never settle for a life in solidarity; exiled from everything he so desperately wanted. *This is not over.*

"Cassidy...do you, um, still *feel* him?" I regretted the question as soon as it spilled from my lips.

I despised myself for my jealousy, for the feeling of inadequacy. *I could've ended it all that day, but I couldn't bring myself to deliver a fatal blow.*

A lump formed in my throat as Cassidy bowed her head.

"I'm scared..." Cassidy's voice was barely a whisper. "Jax is angry."

FIVE

Cassidy

There are some things I could not tell Logan. Things I tried hard not to acknowledge myself. Like right now, Jax was having hard, angry sex with Alyiah. I could not let my husband know that lurking deep within me was a small flicker of jealousy.

I knew my envy was unwarranted; I had everything I wanted, everything I *chose* right here. Yet, the possessive and envious niggle gnawed at my insides. Every time I felt him consummate with her, allowing her to assume the role of his *chosen* mate, my envy of her superseded all logic and rationale. Jax was entitled to happiness and a fresh start. After all, I had ignored the Elders. But my decision to let him live was selfish. My inability to let him go forever. I knew he would be neither happy nor content. *Unless Jax gets what he wants.*

I sensed his departure from the battlefield after my decision that day. I felt him push against it as he increased the distance between us. My body ached for him, yet my mind and my heart were too preoccupied in ensuring Logan's recovery.

Sat at his bedside in the hospital wing, I felt like a fraud. My guilt and longing for his brother plagued me. I felt empty and hollow. Despite everything, I missed Jax.

Twelve weeks after the battle, I discovered I was pregnant with Logan's child. That was my wake-up call. I had to ignore Jax and the feelings he evoked. I was a mother now, a wife and *Queen*.

Ever since, I have tried to bury my connection to Jax. My intent was to focus solely on Logan - the brother who I chose as my soulmate. I wanted to put all my efforts into protecting our child. No one, neither the kingdom's citizens nor the Elders, ever questioned our son's father. *Or at least not openly.*

Yet, despite the time and distance, our *scissa amor vinculum* bond still held strong. Incredibly rare, the broken love bond was something the three of us shared. Only severed in the event of one of their deaths. It had been the cause of the war, the reason I could not decide. Both princes were my soulmates.

Cassidy's War had become a permanent blot on the kingdom of Eyre's history. A stubborn stain on my soul that I could never erase. Innocent blood spilled and families divided. All because I could not choose which of the Princes my heart most desired.

Sleep evaded me. Each night brought wounded cries and the silence of death. I was haunted by the memories of Logan's dismembered hand, his fingers still clutching his sword, laying on the ground among the other bodies that littered the battlefield like discarded trash. I could not fix my mistakes; I had been too reluctant to make a choice and refused to take responsibility for our fates. *I deserve to suffer.*

Even now, my indecision clouded my legacy. The people of Eyre had been correct to doubt me. Only one prince's victory was expected; however, they both survived. I could not let either of them perish. I could not watch Logan die at the hands of this brother. Nor could I let the Elders dispatch Jax like a criminal.

"Cassidy, you are mine."

My heart raced, and goosebumps pricked my skin. Only once before had Jax contacted me telepathically. Usually, I only heard his lamenting thoughts like silent whispers in the dead of night. Our most vulnerable moments. It was always jarring to hear his sorrowful thoughts. It sickened me to learn of his plot of revenge; to return one day and stake his claim on everything he believed to be his. Myself included.

"Cass... he is never coming back here. He can never get to you, or *us.*" Logan's voice purred, his lips fluttering against the top of my head. His strong, muscular arms released me when Felix cried once more; no longer pacified by milk. My head snapped in his directions, meeting his protective and stony glare.

"He will *never* take what is mine." Logan said as he got to his feet and reached for Felix. Taking him into his arms, the ear-splitting wails of our son ceased. "Get some rest, *my Queen.* We can talk about this later."

Logan's lips descended upon my own, kissing me with a passion that left me breathless. Reminding me our love that was deeper than any bond.

"Cassidy, I will *never* let him get close enough to you, or our child, to pose any threat."

I was silent while the two people I loved disappeared out of sight. They were everything I wanted, more than I deserved.

Why do I still long for Jax?

SIX

My hands were trembling as I held on tightly to the pink and white plastic stick in my hand. The bright pink lines glaring up at me from my lap as my mother perched on the edge of the free-standing bath beside me. My stomach clenched, and I wrapped my other hand around it instinctively. *I am pregnant.*

A fact that filled me with more fear than joy. It evoked a fierce protectiveness and anxiety that I had never experienced before. The more I stared at the pregnancy test before me, the louder and clearer Jax's threats reverberated in my head. *"I will not hesitate to plunge my blade through your infant's heart."* It made my blood run cold and my heart freeze like solid ice.

"Cass? Sweetpea?" My mom's voice soothed, her arms enveloping me as I felt my silent tears roll down my cheeks. Wrapped in her warm embrace, I could no longer contain my sobs as they wracked through my body.

"Sweetheart... you will make an exceptional mother," she cooed; her soft, delicate fingertips stroking my arm. "Your father will be so proud of you, and Logan will be beside himself when they learn of this news!"

I stifled my sobs in her shoulder as another powerful wave of guilt flooded through me. I had kept Logan in the dark with my suspicions. He deserved to hear it first; instead, I told Mom. Not only did she know me better than anyone else, she had a duty to keep patient confidentiality. My mom was the leading midwife of Estoria. She took great pride in honoring her vow to protect her patient's secrets. For now, she would keep mine—she *had* to.

"I want to keep this a secret..." My words were muffled by the fabric of her chunky-knit cardigan. Telling Logan required the right moment; I felt her embrace deepen as she planted a tender kiss on my forehead.

"Of course..." she whispered. "I am sworn to secrecy, but darling, this *is* great news. King Logan will be so happy." Her fingers raked through my hair, each silky tendril slipping through them. "Sweetheart, I understand your fear, but I'll support you completely, both as your midwife and mother." She paused, pulling away to look at me.

"We need to know how far along you are. I'll arrange some tests and a scan..." Her voice drifted from my consciousness. My mind already creating scenarios where I tell Logan this news.

When will I tell him? How will he react? I knew he would be happy, but the timing was all wrong. He was on a mission to restore the Kingdom to its original state—safe, united and prosperous. During the day, he attended important meetings. Discussing the future with the Elders and leaders of neighboring kingdoms. *How will a child fit into his demanding schedule?*

I had learned the hard way that being royalty, *the Queen of Xeyiera,* brought about its own issues. Burdened with very little responsibilities, gifted with plenty of time to fill. *Burdened with hours of boredom.*

I hated meandering the castle; I had explored it all. My ambition to explore the world beyond Eyre conflicted with royal life. I had become exactly what I had been opposed to all my life - a caged bird. Isolated for hours upon hours. Logan's fear kept me locked in here; his love held me prisoner.

A pang in my chest, a knot tightened in my stomach. Another reason I yearn for Jax. *He's free; I'm not.* I shook my head, annoyed with myself. *My freedom is a small price to pay. I am lucky Logan is alive.*

I sighed as I walked past Flynn's room. Now he was part of Logan's Royal Guard. He was no longer around to distract me from my surmounting loneliness. Tasked with recruiting and training loyal guards, he was also too busy for me these days. His husband Jace was busy working in my father's Blacksmiths. The demand for swords and shields multiplied with the growing number of guards.

Melody prioritized school, leaving little time for me. Her career options outside Fic hinged on exam results exceeding distinctions. Knowing she preferred being here rather than at school, I couldn't prioritize my boredom over her future.

It was rare that mom was around these days. Her demanding position took her far and wide across Eyre. So, it was me. *Alone and bored out of my brain.*

I scrubbed a spot of ink stained on the beige stone floor of the bedroom. It was ironic, when I lived at home, I hated such obligatory chores. Yet here I was choosing to do them, even though there was no need. We had staff for such duties.

"What do you think you are doing, my Queen?" My scrubbing was interrupted by Lottie's exclamation. She snatched it from my grasp, casting a look of annoyance my way as she threw it into the bucket. The force of her throw sent soapy water to splash over the rim. I spent most of my time with the castle's staff, the maids, and the cooks. Though none of them could be considered a *friend,* Lottie was the closest I would have.

"I need to keep busy." I mumbled, slumping into a sitting position on the floor and crossing my arms over my chest. "I am bored, Lottie... lonely and fed-up. Why can't I help?"

Lottie helped me to my feet. "Cos' you're *the Queen!*" Her tone was annoyed, but her face was soft with a small smile. She frantically brushed off the non-existent lint from the bottom of my lace dress.

"A Queen does *not* get on their knees and scrub the floor like a lowly maid." She sighed. "If you need to keep yourself busy, why don't you have a baby? Or read a book? It's not like you don't have an entire library full of them, or a handsome husband to bed."

I lowered my head, biting my lip. I needed to tell someone this secret before it exploded like a ticking time bomb. "Lottie... I'm-" I saw her eyes bulge, without the need to finish my sentence. Her smile stretched from ear to ear, revealing her slightly askew teeth.

"My Queen, that's fantastic! The King must be so thrilled!" she squealed, embracing me while jumping on the spot. Suddenly she stopped, her face frowning at me. "Another reason *you* should not be scrubbing floors!"

"Lottie... um, I haven't told him yet." My words were quiet as she pulled away from me. She shot me a quizzical glare, questioning almost. "I only found out this morning," I added hastily.

"Only found out what?" My head snapped up at the sound of his voice, *Jax.* I ignored him. Jax, of all people, could *not* find out before Logan. *"Tell me now Cassidy!"*

The anger in his voice was undeniable. His thoughts already revealed that he had guessed. Unwilling to accept that his worst fear was about to be confirmed. *"That motherfucker... you're pregnant, aren't you?"*

"There you are, Cass... *my queen."* Logan's voice reverberated in the room, startling me. Lottie scarpered, giving me a small smile over her shoulder as she left. "I have been looking for you." His arms wrapped around me from behind, his lips nuzzling the nape of my neck.

"I visited Mother," I replied, tilting my head to look at him. "I was bored." Finding myself biting back the true nature of my visit. I could feel Jax listening to our conversation.

"Already lying to him, I see," Jax said as I pictured his smug grin. I was giving him ammunition, fueling his determination to seek revenge. *"That's never a good sign."*

"Why... why were you looking for me?" I summoned all my strength to push them both from my thoughts; feeling relieved when my connection with Jax finally severed. "Um... s-should I be worried?"

Logan's chuckle sent his hot breath tingling against my neck. His lips returned to the base as he kissed his way up to my mouth.

"Can't a husband want to see his wife? Kiss her? *Make love* to her without having a reason?" A smile curved his lips, crinkling his eyes, as he faced me. "I want to spend some time with you. I have been so busy lately that I have neglected the most important person in my life."

I felt his hand slide beneath the lace hem of my dress. Sliding my underwear to the side and tenderly smoothing his fingertips over my slit. My knees weakened; my body molded against his as he slid a finger inside.

"I was thinking we could go to *our* lake. So that we could have some *real* privacy."

I inhaled the fragrance of the wild blooms as they danced in the gentle breeze; their strong floral notes filled my lungs. The soft whispers of the long grass caressed my bare skin as my legs pushed through it as I neared the edge of the lake. Instantly, the calmness of our sacred place washed over me.

Even after all these years, this was the one place that still felt safe. Free from the scars of battle and the stains of innocent blood. Before the war, before I met either of the Silverthorne princes, I would come here to think. Or not think at all. An escape from the mundanity of my life. The only spot in Fic left completely untouched and nature left to thrive. I could pretend I was somewhere else in Xeyiera, anywhere other than trapped here.

Though I could only come here escorted by Logan these days, I did not mind. This was where we first met, first kissed. Two strangers succumbing to their instinctive desire. Like magnets, we were both compelled to each other; unknowing at the time how our futures would unfold. Never did I expect that the mysterious stranger would be a Prince. Nor that I would be a Queen.

My eyes glanced over to my left looking for something, a small smile crept across my face the moment I found it. The tree Logan pinned me against, his hands holding my thigh as it wrapped around his waist. The sensation of feeling his rigid shaft push against my core. The fire that surged through me, begging for more.

"I always wondered what would have happened had Flynn not interrupted us." Logan grinned, brushing the back of his fingertips against my cheek. Plucking a loose curl that had escaped my fancy hairstyle Lottie had styled that morning. Our bodies were so close together, the pull of the bond intensified. Both of us inching closer until my nose brushed his and Logan's hot breath flitted across my lips.

There was always a spark the moment our lips touched. Setting my skin abuzz with electricity as his fingertips crept beneath my blouse.

"Me too." I murmured, his hands taking hold of mine as he guided us towards it.

"Perhaps it might have gone something like this." He smirked.

My back slammed against the trunk; his body pressed against mine. The throb of his restrained manhood pinned me in place as his hands caressed my breasts. Letting out a deep growl as he pinched my taut nipples.

Logan's hands fumbled at the buttons. His iron hand made it more difficult, yet he never let it stop him. Delight and lust filled his eyes the moment he saw them spilling out of the top of the emerald green bra. Fuller and heavier than they had ever been. The blissful relief as he unfastened it immediately replaced with intense pleasure. Cupping each one simultaneously, drawing them into his greedy mouth.

Unable to stifle my moans, allowing them to resonate in the silence, echoing in the empty clearing that surrounded the lake. A crow abandoned its perch from within the tree, cawing in its disgruntlement. I felt Logan's mouth curl into a mischievous grin as he slid one hand beneath my skirt. His fingers explored my silky thighs until his fingertips found my aching slit.

I drew my leg around his waist, inviting his fingers to explore deeper as he rolled a nipple between his teeth. A ripple of ecstasy danced along my spine, driving my nails to dig into his flesh. I had never experienced such intense pleasure. *This must be a pregnancy thing.*

In an instant, Logan's brown eyes were staring into mine. His hands stilled and his jaw dropped. *Shit, this wasn't how I planned to tell him.*

"Logan…" I whispered, fearing he was angry. "I should have told you earlier… it's why I visited my mom…I-" My words were swallowed by his kiss. All teeth and tongues, fueled by passion, Logan pulled me down to the soft bed of grass.

"I…love…you…Cassidy." He gasped between kisses as they trailed down my body. Momentarily pausing when he reached my stomach. Even though it was not swollen yet, it would soon look like I had swallowed a beach ball. Just the thought made me feel self-conscious.

Planting kisses all over my abdomen, Logan's eyes never left mine. "You are beautiful, my Queen. You will always be perfect in my eyes."

"Even when I look like a plump goose?"

Logan chuckled, "you'll look even more delicious." He smirked, slipping my skirt and lace underwear down my legs.

My back arched as his tongue lapped against my slit. His tongue teasing my sensitive nub before driving it deep inside my entrance. I clutched at fistfuls of long grass as wave after wave of pleasure crashed through me. Completely uncaring of how loud my moans become as I neared my orgasm.

"I am the luckiest person in the whole of Xeyiera." His voice filled my head.

Threading my fingers into his hair, I pulled his face back up to mine. I could taste the tangy sweetness of myself on his lips and tongue, which made me deepen the kiss even more.

"Me too," I replied, my hand finding his metal limb, pushing it down to my core. The cold bite of the metal as two fingers stretched my entrance made me gasp out loud. "I love you Logan…"

The smile broadened across his face, creasing the corners of his glassy eyes. "I still can't believe you are carrying my child." He slid his metal limb deeper, enjoying the sight of me as I bit my bottom lip, stifling my moans.

"You are so perfect." He brought his mouth back down against mine. "I will always protect you, Cassidy. You are mine, always."

Guilt punched a hole in my chest as I blocked my thoughts from Logan. Before my eyes, Logan's face twisted into Jax's. Watching as he took his position back between my legs once more. Memories of similar scenarios with Jax flooded my mind as my orgasm ripped through my body. I should not be thinking of Jax right now.

"There is no point in lying to yourself." Jax's voice purred, *"Nor is there any shame in fantasizing over your true soulmate."*

I bit my lip hard, riding the wave of pleasure that coursed through me. My stomach twisted into knots. This is so wrong. I felt Jax smirk, enjoying the turmoil that spiraled in my thoughts.

"Cass, we both know you chose Logan out of guilt, not love." Jax continued, his internal voice sounded breathless. *"We both know it is me who should be there, fucking you... making you cum over and over."*

Logan's rigid member replaced his metallic fingers, his lips crashing down on mine as he thrust in slow, precise movements. Savoring the tightness of my walls as they clamped around him, a perfectly snug fit. Instinctively, my fingers clawed deep grooves along his spine. Jax used to love that. It would always spur him on to increase his pace. The fantasy of Jax overwhelmed me. *What the fuck is wrong with me?*

My hands froze when Logan hissed in pain. *Shit.* I murmured an apology, knowing I had scratched him deep. Feeling the slickness of blood beneath my fingertips. *How could I have gotten so carried away?*

As my eyes adjusted to Logan's, I felt another stab of guilt pierce my heart. *"No Jax, you're wrong... I love Logan, this... this is just because of the bond."* I added firmly, feeling a snap as Jax severed the connection. His anger resonated for several moments in his wake.

"Logan, I'm so sorry..." I murmured as my fingers traced over his wounds. My healing ability repairing the damage I had inflicted. "I, um, got a little too carried away."

Logan's eyes darkened, unable to contain the lust that was brimming inside them. He drove his hips against mine, sinking his shaft deeper into my core as his lips crashed against mine. I writhed and bucked against him, my hands clutching at anything and everything. I could feel his pleasure, his need for release, but I could feel something else, too. *Anger.*

"Who do you really want, Cass? Me or Jax?"

I choked back a sob. "You, Logan." I wrapped my arms around his neck, feeling his tense muscles loosen, comforted by my words. "It always has been, and always will be, you."

SEVEN

PRESENT DAY—*Twelve Hours Earlier*

Logan

Laughter filled the air, childish and high-pitched. It echoed loudly in the Map Room as Felix played 'battle' with the small wooden figurines. Each one represented a soldier on the scale model of Estoria. Figurines that had at one point represented my strategy in the notorious 'Cassidy's War'.

Every time I looked at them, flashbacks of the battle would flood my thoughts. The horrific sights and haunting sounds tortured me until I had to leave the room. Yet today I had to be here; I had to prepare. *Jax is coming, and he is not alone.*

Flynn and Esan, my most trusted guards, were transfixed as Felix played with the figurines. Slamming them down on the table, bashing them together and chuckling with glee. The pair of them were quick to join in, fueling his already hyper imagination. He was nearly three; war was beyond his grasp. Too young to be thrust into the shitstorm Jax would unleash if he entered Estoria. *Jax wants revenge and will stop at nothing to get it.*

Over the past few months, I had heard whispers of him gathering allies and trying to build an army. Stubborn in his belief that the throne and Cassidy should be his. Jax had a mission; to claim it all. I had spies keeping track of his whereabouts, reporting his latest moves. He was scraping together the unlikeliest of people for support, from witches and pirates to dodgy traders. The most harrowing was the necromancer. *The Phantom.*

Supposedly living anonymously in the shadows, he was a specter every child was taught to fear. Jax had always had a morbid fascination with him, his plight to raise our mother from beyond the grave. My father had been quick to shoot down Jax's idyllic notion, set on turning Jax away from his recent obsession. *"That is not the way life works. Your mother's soul is at peace. We do not know what may become of it once The Phantom has his evil grip on it."*

The moment I learned The Phantom was involved in Jax's plan; I started my research. I required knowledge of our opponents. What the potential consequences would be should Jax's plan be successful.

I had scoured every book in the castle's library, but it was nothing but vague scraps of information. None of it held any stock. Hearsay and speculation. Nothing that would help me keep Estoria safe. *Nothing that would help me protect my family.*

"You will not find the answers you are looking for in any book." Elder Jeremiah said, his voice startled me. Immediately drawing my attention away from the book on my desk. I slammed it closed, not wanting the Elders to get involved. *At least not yet.*

The orbs of white shone like beacons against the dark depths of his robe, staring into my soul. "Especially about The Phantom."

"How do you know-" I cut myself off. Not only would my thoughts have given me away, but I should have known the Elders would keep tabs on my brother's whereabouts.

"The Phantom was an Elder once..." Brother Jeremiah spoke, his voice solemn. "Though his gift led him astray, there was a time when he was known as Elder Zeke."

The silence that followed seemed to hang thick and heavy in the atmosphere. My mind whirring with questions but unable to voice them. *Elder Zeke?* Legends and myths have always cited seven, not eight, Elders. *How is this possible?*

Elder Jeremiah let out a low rumble of laughter, closing the gap between us. "History's victors shape its story. You will not find it documented in any book, but Elder Zeke was, *is,* my brother."

I felt my eyes pop out of my head in shock, but before I could voice my thoughts, Elder Jeremiah continued talking. "There were eight divinely crafted beings who initially started the world's creation. Created by angels and Gods, and scattered far and wide. Lacking direction, we searched for one another, combining our talents to create a livable world."

Elder Jeremiah paused as he righted himself, gliding soundlessly across the room until he reached the Map of Xeyiera hanging on the wall to my left. It still adorned the pins from the troll sightings; a reminder of the almost-catastrophic diversion my younger sister, Demi, had planned. I could never bring myself to remove them. Those miniscule pin holes had damaged the tapestry, one that had hung in the same spot for centuries. *Just like Demi's actions will forever blemish Xeyiera's history and landscape,* I thought.

"The Gods were not kind. Their mission for this untamed world was harsh. Full of monsters beyond your wildest nightmares. Most of us were alone, but not me. Zeke was like a shadow, following me from one end of the world to the other."

Elder Jeremiah's hands brushed over the map. "We were brothers because he was designed with the same angel's grace as me. The closest thing to a mother we had, if you could call her that. Only it was not the Gods who created him, but the Devil himself."

I twisted my chair to look at Elder Jeremiah; the only person alive privy to such intimate details.

Zeke would provide equilibrium. Neither one of us could survive without the other. We were a careful balance of dark and light, good and *evil*. The true scope of his abilities upon humanity's emergence, exposing his direct connection to the Devil."

Elder Jeremiah stared silently at the map for a few moments. "These humans could love and think independently, free to do as they please to build a society among them." He sighed, turning his back on the map as if it evoked a painful memory. "It soon became clear that humans *craved* chaos."

I nodded, though I did not understand. He bowed his cloaked head. "One day, a human died as a result and his lover begged for us to bring him back. We all felt her broken heart, the swell of her stomach revealing an unborn child. Her grief inspired us to lay out rules, strict ways of living to reduce such chaos."

I nodded, muttering under my breath. "The Rules of Conduct." My head was still spinning with unasked questions, but Elder Jeremiah's glare kept me silent. His internal voice assured me he would answer what I wanted to know in due course.

Elder Jeremiah's cloaked head nodded as my thoughts quietened. "The Gods helped draft such rules, and we were eager to abide by their commands. Zeke and the Devil exploited our distraction to strike a bargain with her. They demanded her first-born child for the resurrection of her lover."

I felt my eyes pop out of my head, but Elder Jeremiah ignored my shock.

"Of course, the rest of us were horrified at this concept. The others begged the Gods to banish Zeke from this world; to take him to the depths of Hell with the Devil himself. But for whatever reason, they refused, forsaking all of us instead." His voice grew even quieter. "We all hate to admit our mistakes, but every one of us has asked Zeke for help at least once in our long, lonely lives."

Elder Jeremiah was quiet, too quiet, as he drew his eyes back to the map. "We Elders avoid human interaction for a reason. Your lives are but a speck of dust compared to ours. Our emotions are stronger than a fickle human's. We watch as you age and perish. We choose not to love, for it is a heartbreak too painful to keep reliving."

In one swift movement, Elder Jeremiah was before me. Images from a distant past filled my mind as his gloved fingers framed my head. The unfolding scene revealed *his* memories.

EIGHT

The sun had not yet set, slashes of red and amber scored the blue sky beyond the rickety wooden window. Yet my attention was diverted elsewhere in the room.

Laid upon the bed, coughing up blood, was a frail woman with a shock of pure white hair. Her wrinkled face contorted with pain as the hacking cough shook her petite frame. I reached for her hand, feeling how ice-cold her skin was to my touch. I saw the agony behind her eyes with each second that passed. She was dying.

Day and night I had insisted on our healers' help; all of them failed to aid in her recovery. No matter how many medicinal concoctions they poured down her throat. Nor the copious amount of herbs burning in a clay pot on her bedside table. There was nothing they could do to reverse the effects of her aging.

My beloved Agatha, deteriorating before my very eyes, talking not to me but to the Gods she was soon to join. I could not allow it - I did not want to face this world without her. Yet as time ticked by, her vital organs failed her. *Soon she will become nothing more than a cherished memory.*

The thought of her lifeless body buried in the soil made my blood run cold. Her decaying corpse, devoured by maggots and other wildlife, caused bile to rise in my throat. *I can't let that happen to her.*

Instinctively, my mind reached out to him, to my brother Zeke. *He is the only one who can help.* It had been quite some time since I had seen him. I knew what would become of her, that she would not be the Agatha I loved. Yet I could not bear to live without seeing her face every day. I would pay the price, whatever it is, so that the love of my life would walk beside me for all eternity.

"Brother, I need your help." I pleaded, trying to open our telepathic connection that had remained dormant for many years. *"Please, I beg you."*

Silence was all that greeted me. My misery slowly encompassed me as I watched through blurry eyes. The rise and fall of her chest slowed, her last few raspy breaths taken. I clutched her hand tightly. It was only when the time came for her last gasp of air, rattling her frail lungs, did I allow my tears to fall.

My sorrow was soon replaced by anger. *Why had Zeke not come to my aid?* I lashed out at the few furnishings in the room, throwing the chair I had been sitting on through the window. Glass shattered like a million stars. Glittering in the last few rays of the sunshine as they scattered the floor below. My own breaths were heavy with anguish. My rage was uncontrollable, growling as I sought something else to unleash the fury of my broken heart upon.

"Brother, I am here." Zeke's voice said coolly in my mind, feeling his hand on my shoulder before seeing his cloaked form. *"You know the consequences of using my gift,"* he continued. *"You must sacrifice another for her resurrection. The younger the soul, the more life I can breathe back into her."*

I knew it was wrong, but the Gods had already forsaken us. I no longer cared how heinous an act it was. That night, under the cover of darkness, I found my sacrifice. Its wails pierced the silence, and I followed the noise until it was cradled in my arms, tucked in a pastel blue shawl. Shushing the babe, I brought it back to my beloved's bedside. Zeke was already there waiting, with candles lit in a circle around her bed. Large black dahlia petals scattered over her body. A silver blade on the bedside table beside the clay bowl that had been emptied of the cremated herbs.

A lump formed in my throat as the babe in my arms flailed its limbs, as if it was trying to escape its impending fate. *"Are you sure you can do this, brother?"* Zeke asked, his fingertips wrapping around the hilt of the blade. Dragging it across the surface, leaving a deep groove in its wake. The sound of the metal scraping against the wood sent a shiver down my spine. *"There is no going back."* Zeke warned. I shook my head, watching in silence as his fist wrapped around the blade's handle. His other hand reaching for the child in my arms.

I nodded once, knowing I should shut my eyes once I handed the child over to him. But the babe shrieked; a deafening and heart-wrenching squeal that held my attention. The cries were replaced by a slick, wet sound. Blood trickled from the babe's throat into the clay pot. My stomach churned, but I was too mesmerized to look away. Morbid curiosity held me captive as I watched the life-force of this unknown child fill the bowl.

Guilt squeezed my lungs, my mind conjuring images of the child's distraught parents. Imagining their pain and sorrow at the discovery of their newborn snatched from its crib.

Zeke's bloodied fingers snapped before my face, breaking me out of my dream-like trance. I could hear a raspy whisper, his voice almost unrecognizable after decades of silence.

"Leave now brother. She will return to you soon."

I made my way out of the room; forcing one foot in front of the other. I gave my brother one last look over my shoulder. Zeke was fussing over the lifeless corpse of Agatha, muttering incohesive words. The clay bowl rested in one hand while his other smeared the blood across her porcelain skin. Drawing symbols, *runes*, over her body as he performed the ritual.

Zeke ripped open the buttons on her shirt, revealing her bare breasts. "What are you doing?" I demanded, my hands balled into fists, disgusted by his disrespect.

Zeke did not look up, nor did he stop as his hands continued to paint more symbols on her bare skin. *"If you are going to stay, brother, please be quiet."* Zeke's internal voice chided. I stood frozen in place, my attention drifting over to the table where the babe was silent.

The blanket now bore dark rust-colored stains. Only then did I realize the child I had sacrificed was actually a girl, drapped in a hand-me-down, threadbare blanket from an older sibling. Not only had I had taken an innocent life, one so young and so full of potential in my selfish desire to heal my broken heart, I had also destroyed her family's lives. *I am a monster.*

I squeezed my eyes shut and swallowed the bitter taste that filled my mouth; trying desperately to ignore the pit that was opening up in my stomach. Without realizing, I was back beside her on the bed, her hand ice-cold in mine. *I need you, Agatha.*

Keeping my eyes closed, I waited. The silence deepened in the room, growing heavy and ominous. The incessant tick as the grandfather clock's pendulum swung. *Tick, tick, tick.* Each second echoing louder than the last, heightening my fear and intensifying my regret. I was afraid I had surrendered a child in vain as Agatha's body lay still.

Suddenly, I felt her slender fingers tightening around mine. "J-Jerry?" Agatha whispered. My heart fluttered hearing her voice once more. "Jerry, what-" A harsh, barking cough interrupted her, "what happened?"

My gaze locked onto her, noticing the sparkle of youth dart across her cerulean-blue eyes. Watching every line and wrinkle on her face fade away; transforming back into the young woman who had stolen my heart. Full pink lips curved into a breathtaking smile, her eyes piercing my soul. She reached out to me. Her underarms no longer sagged, and her exposed breasts defied gravity once more.

"My love," she whispered, I leaned forward to kiss her, feeling the wetness of the infant's blood against my skin. Nausea threatened, yet I needed confirmation. *Is this real? Had Agatha truly returned to me?*

"How do you feel, Agatha?" My words danced across her parted lips.

"Incredible," she purred, kissing me once more. "I feel *alive.*"

NINE

Jax

Had I not been drunk myself, I would have been from inhaling the fumes that radiated off the man before me. *He is a pirate. What did I expect?*

Black, matted hair hung limp beneath his red bandana. His youthful face was a map of scars and battle wounds. *He is not much older than me.* Yet he had a mouth full of black and decaying teeth. Life on the sea had come with some health hazards.

I could see his lips moving, but his words were not registering. I had heard too much of his exaggerated, bullshit tales of his 'victories'. I was not here to listen to him blathering on about his greatest raids. All I wanted was his boats and his crew. Better yet, if I could get the support of the pirates on my side, I would have an advantage over Logan.

"...there is not a man or woman alive who doesn't quiver in fear at the mention of our names since that day!" The man laughed, slamming his empty stein on the table before us. "Another!" he yelled over his shoulder.

I saw my opportunity to speak; the only one that had opened up in the last hour. "So... what do you say, Morgan? Do we have a deal?"

The pirate before me scratched his beard, his arrogance radiated from him as he stared at me. "I still don't see what is in it for me," he replied, leaning back to allow the barmaid to fill his stein once more.

The girl caught my eye, a natural red-head with a smattering of faint freckles over her pale face and piercing green eyes. Her porcelain cheeks flushed a deep crimson when she noticed me staring at her. I thought of Cassidy, the way she had gotten embarrassed, and the hue of her flushed face when she orgasmed. The girl went to leave, but I reached out for her hand, kissing the back of it.

Her green eyes sparkled and a small smile crept across her lips. "Why don't you join me?" I said, "after I have finished up here..." Blushing, she gave me a small nod before returning to her position behind the bar.

"Good luck getting into that one," Morgan cackled, gesturing his head in the girl's direction. "I bet she's tighter than a hangman's knot."

I eyed 'Mad' Morgan, a name given for the shenanigans boasted about in his drunken tales. Not that I believed a word of them, but I believed the reputation of his anger. Morgan's long-time feud with another pirate showcased his *unforgiving* side.

With a long, leather trench-coat, he did not look like the pirates written in the children's tales with wooden legs and parrots on their shoulders. Instead, he had the look of a thug. His black shirt was unbuttoned, revealing a tuft of black, wiry hair covering his muscular body. His jeans were tight around his thick, muscular thighs. Morgan was built like a monster. *Perfect.*

'Mad' Morgan looked more like a murderous villain than a gold-hungry pirate. With the reputation that preceded him, I recognized he would be an ally I needed.

The enemy of my enemy is my friend. Pirates were becoming a bigger problem for my brother, and I was determined to make his life hell before I ended it. I wanted to uncover Morgan's weakness; *leverage* against him to force his cooperation.

'Mad' Morgan leaned forward. "I ain't got time to waste..." He grunted, pushing his chair away from the table. The piercing shriek of wood against wood rang out. Everyone in the tavern looked our way.

"What can *you* offer me in return for my help?" Morgan barked.

I jumped to my feet, squaring up to his challenge. In one swift movement, I slammed down the canvas bag I had kept hidden beneath the table this whole time.

His eyes narrowed. His brow knitted together as he studied the canvas bag. Crimson seeped through the fabric and pooled on the table, along with his spilled ale. "What the fuck is this?" he snarled, reaching for the cutlass attached to his hip.

"It's a present," I replied, crossing my arms in front of my chest. "Open it." I watched Morgan untie the drawstring cord holding the bag closed; enjoying the way his facial features transformed from a scowl into a grin.

"Is this who I think it is?"

I nodded, reaching into the bag and pulling out the severed head of 'Salty' by a tuft of dark, ginger hair. Blood dripped from the severed neck as I held it aloft. Salty's face was forever contorted in pain. I released my grip - the head came tumbling down onto the table. It's blank, glazed stare pointed at Morgan.

"So... do we have a deal?" I repeated my question, receiving only a disgusted look from the bartender. "His life, for your unwavering support."

Morgan nodded, chuckling under his breath as he lifted the head up to his own, checking to see if it was genuine and not some elaborate trick. I reached into the bag to retrieve two more items; a brass pocket watch and a bloodied handkerchief. Inside lay a finger, still adorned with a large gold ring encrusted with small rubies.

"In case you needed more proof," I smirked. "This is all that remains of your *uncle.*"

Morgan's eyes opened wide, dropping the head unceremoniously to the table. Snatching up the bloodied digit, he studied it with wide eyes. The ring was a family heirloom, but now it would act as a talisman of Salty's defeat; a trophy Morgan could wield to command Salty's large band of pirates. Not only had I served him his enemy's head, but I had gifted him more power and ships than he ever thought possible.

His black crooked teeth were exposed in a wide grin, still studying the clammy, blue-gray mottled finger in his hand. He slammed his fist onto the table, crushing the finger. The ring popped off the end, like a cork inside a bottle. The ring clattered, spiraling on the table before falling still with a solid thump.

Without a moment's hesitation, Morgan picked it up. Smearing blood along his middle finger as he slid it on. He outstretched his filthy, bloody hand to me, a smile spanned from ear to ear on his scarred face. I took it, offering him a firm handshake; without a flicker of remorse or disgust. *It's only blood. Soon it will be Logan's.* I would not succumb to sentimentality as I did before.

Morgan stared at me; his judgmental glare cast over me. If I wanted his respect, I had to break away from my royal reputation. After all, I was not a 'pampered prince' any more. I was an outlaw, exiled from the kingdom that should be mine, with nothing to my name. *Without Cassidy by my side.*

"There is one more thing..." I added, snaking my hand through the dead man's hair and lifting it up from the table once more. "This..." I said, shoving the decaying face into Morgan's, "was more than a gesture of goodwill."

"Is that a threat?" Morgan hissed, lunging forward so that his face was inches from mine, a snarl curled on his lips and his foul breath filled my nostrils. Being nose-to-nose, he thought he would intimidate me, but it only made me more determined.

Shaking my head, I replied unflinchingly. "No. It's a *promise*. Should you try to fuck me over, this is the fate you will wish you had."

Morgan gulped as the figure of The Phantom materialized in the doorframe. Bringing with him the stench of rotten flesh. I shoved the head into Morgan's stomach. "Are we clear?"

He batted the head away, sending it toppling off the table and rolling to a stop at the barmaid's feet. She shrieked in horror, a terrified expression etched into her pretty doll-like face. She reminded me of Cassidy so much; not in looks, but her innocence and purity captivated me. I *had* to have her.

I felt an icy hand on my shoulder before his words filtered into my mind. *"Business before pleasure,"* The Phantom warned, snapping the fingers of his other hand before my face to remove me from my trance-like gaze. I was never one to take heed of warnings, but he was right. In those few moments I had spent staring at the barmaid, Morgan had already backed away from the table.

"Get your men ready. We will be leaving at sunrise," I told him. "We set sail for the furthest point on the map."

I noticed the head had disappeared from the floor. The Phantom offered the canvas bag back to Morgan. *"Don't forget to take your present, Captain."* He had a way of speaking without using his mouth. Projecting his thoughts for all to hear, the black orbs in the eyeholes of his mask stared at Morgan. *"Jax will not be so merciful with you."*

Less than an hour later, I had her. Pressed up against the wall of the toilet cubicle, our mouths locked into frantic kisses as my hands fumbled to remove her jeans. I growled, my frustration getting the better of me.

"Mmm, Yeah... like that." Cassidy's voice melted into my ears as if she were before me. *Thrust.* *"yes... yes!"* *Thrust.* *"Don't stop Logan."* *Thrust.* My teeth clenched together as the anger simmered beneath my skin. With every thrust, I felt the pressure building up inside of her, heard every moan that escaped her lips.

"Get those fucking jeans off." I barked, stepping back and watching her undress. "And your shirt."

The girl, whose name I could not remember, trembled as she unfastened the buttons and slid off her jeans. Unstable on her feet, her arms wrapped around her body as she stood before me, naked. She disliked the way my gaze scrutinized every inch of her.

Her complexion was too pale and mottled with freckles. Her red hair flowed past her shoulders, the tips brushing against her perky nipples. It was only her innocence that bore any semblance to Cassidy, but it didn't matter. I needed to fuck, to feel my release, to forget Logan existed.

I craved a connection with Cassidy. Fucking someone else made it easier to pretend I was the one taking her to the edge, not my brother.

"What was your name again?" I asked, my hands pulling at her waist, pushing her forward so her ass was in the air, her wet slit waiting for me.

"Gwen," she gasped, feeling my solid cock thrust into her. 'Mad' Morgan was correct in his assumption. She was fucking tight. My thick shaft stretching her walls, gripping every inch of my thick, throbbing uncut length as I drove it in deep. The sensation of my foreskin being pulled back to reveal the purple engorged head evoked a low growl to unfurl from my throat.

I moaned, my hands squeezing her nipples hard, keeping a steady rhythm. "Soon I will bend you over my *fucking* throne." *Thrust.* "You can keep me occupied while the Queen is busy birthing me heirs." *Moan.* I slid a finger into her exposed ass. *If her pussy is this this tight, her ass will make me shoot my load in less than a fucking minute.*

Feeling Cassidy's breaths tighten in my own chest, on the verge of her climax, I spat on her rosebud entrance. Driving my cock deep into it without any warning. Gwen cried out, but did not dare beg me to stop. She soon succumbed to the pleasure.

Feeling Cassidy's breaths tighten in my chest, I increased my pace; allowing Cassidy's moans to drown out Gwen's in my ears. Anger seethed through my veins, my hands acting on impulse as they wrapped around Gwen's throat. I fucked her hard, my grasp tightening, squeezing hard, as Cassidy's orgasm ripped through my body.

Gwen gasped and choked before going limp. It was then I realized I had gone too far. Releasing her, I watched as her body crumpled to the floor. Cum shot from my tip in thick white ropes over her lifeless body. I shuddered, panting heavily. My hand milked my pulsating shaft until all my load was spent.

One less heart to break. I thought, grabbing a fistful of her hair to mop up the cum that dripped from the tip of my cock before shoving it back inside my jeans. Thinking of Alyiah as I stared down at Gwen. I had no intention of moving on. Despite what Alyiah may think and the lies I plied her with, there would only ever be one mate for me. My soulmate - Cassidy.

I will not stop until I get her back. No matter the cost.

TEN

Cassidy

A brush of ice-cold metal grazed my nipple before his hot mouth clamped over it. The sensation evoked eruptions like fireworks within. Breathless from my last orgasm, I still yearned for more. His other hand trailed down to my slit; his fingers teasing with slow strokes along the entrance.

"Logan..." I panted, feeling his suction grow stronger around my nipple, my back arching off of the bed to meet his hungry mouth. When he released, I felt his lips form a sneaky grin. His hands gripped my hips tightly.

I froze, self-conscious about the excess skin that hung on my body. That small padding of fat that lingered after giving birth to Felix. After all these years and exercise regimes, it still bothered me that those rolls of fat would not budge. I pushed his hands away automatically.

"Cassidy," Logan murmured, "when will you accept that you are beautiful?" He planted delicate kisses along the faint silver stretch marks that blemished my skin. "Each of these should be seen as trophies. The miracle of life you grew inside you... *My* son." His kisses drew over my hips. "I love the curves of your body..." A growl resonated from his chest. "What you may see as flaws are *sexy*..." He did not finish his sentence, instead his stiff fingers brushed my clit, causing me to squirm beneath him. My hands clutching fistfuls of his hair while splaying my legs as wide as possible.

I felt his fingers tease my entrance; their touch happily welcomed as he pushed them in deeper. I squealed. Another orgasm building once more. Like a pressurized canister ready to explode. *I want him. I need him.*

I shut my eyes as my orgasm rocked through my body, my loud moans bounced off the stone walls of the castle. Yet when I opened them, I was no longer in our bedroom in the castle; instead, I was in a dingy red-brick cubicle. Jealousy prickled inside as I realized what was happening. The porcelain skinned girl inhaled sharply, her red hair clutched tightly into the fist of my host. Her face was only visible as a slither of a side profile.

My eyes slid down to her bare ass cheeks, spread wide as Jax's shaft thrust deep into her rosebud. I could feel his pleasure, could hear his thoughts as he slammed his hips into her buttocks. Envy spread through me, the want to feel the pleasure this girl was feeling.

"Your ass is mine." Jax's thought seethed, *"I am glad Logan has not been there since... I want that to remain one part of your body untainted by his touch."*

I scowled, breaking the connection. Frustrated and angry with myself, allowing this sacred and intimate moment to be hijacked by Jax. Yet my body ached for his touch, to feel that sensation of his hard shaft deep inside my tight ass. I allowed myself to think of that night; to reminisce about the thrill of the two princes fighting for my affection. My lust spurred on by their jealousy to give me the greatest orgasm. But now, as Logan slid his rigid member into me, I knew I needed more.

"Logan..." I murmured, sliding out from underneath him, getting onto my hands and knees and raising my ass in the air. "I want you to..." At first, I could hear the hesitation in his thoughts as he stroked the tip against my rosebud entrance. "Yes..." I purred, pushing against it, feeling it stretch a little. "Fuck, yes..."

Logan groaned as he sank his shaft inside. His fingertips dug into my flesh; the coldness of his iron hand sent shivers along my spine. "Cass..." he moaned over and over. His voice deepened, becoming huskier each time. "Fuck..."

I bucked against him, putting all of my weight on my left hand so that I could slide my own fingers into my warmth. Instantly enjoying the sensation of both entrances being stretched. In my mind, I replayed the moment both of them took me, filling both holes at the same time. A startled cry escaped my lips. My toes curled as my orgasm tore through me.

Jax's anger only intensified the pleasure. I craved for another. I wanted him to keep going until my body was sore and ached. Logan purred at my thought, his shaft twitching before his load erupted deep within my tight hole.

"I will do anything my Queen commands." Logan's thoughts echoed yet he panted almost incoherently, "but Cass, we have never... the first time..."

He collapsed on the bed beside me; his cum trickling down the backs of my legs and the insides of my thighs. "Fucking hell..."

"*What the fuck.*" Jax's voice boomed, snapping out of my temporary high. "*I told you; your ass is mine. You are mine.*"

I gritted my teeth. "*I do not belong to you. You have that slut, or Alyiah, for your needs.*" The anger that oozed in my words was genuine, unable to disguise my jealousy. Though I was more infuriated at how my body reacted to him being with someone else. I hated myself and the green-eyed monster within. A monster conjured from our bond that destroyed all sense of reason and rationality. I despised the way I had used Logan to taunt Jax.

Deep down, I enjoyed Jax's rage bubbling inside me. His fury made his actions more brutal and barbaric. I wanted him to hurt the girl; to make her feel pain rather than pleasure. *All because she was not me.*

A snippet of Jax's vision appeared before my eyes, of the girl face down on the white-tiled floor. Limp and covered with his cum. I shuddered in horror. My sadistic, impulsive wish had been granted. *I am a monster.*

Sleep eluded me for the rest of the night: haunted by the image of the girl, conflicted by my emotions. *Was what I have with Logan, what I really want?* My stomach twisted into knots; the thought of not being beside him. No longer wrapped in his arms where I felt safe. *I love Logan;* I told myself firmly. *It is only this stupid bond that makes me crave Jax.*

I snuggled against Logan's chest, feeling it rise and fall, as he slept blissfully unaware of my doubts. I reminded myself of all the things I loved about him–forcing myself to acknowledge the girl's death at Jax's hands. Yet despite this evil deed, the bond between us held stronger than ever before. *I can't keep feeling like this, but what can I do?*

"*Flynn?*" I whispered, trying to open the telepathic connection with him. It had been a while since we had used it. I needed someone to talk to; someone who understood my turmoil, who had been there through it all. Over time, we had grown apart. *Would he really understand?*

He answered straight away. "*Cass? What's wrong?*"

"*Nothing...*" I replied. *He is loyal to Logan, part of his fucking personal guard. Whatever I say would get back to Logan.* I sighed, suddenly feeling isolated. "*Sorry.*"

"*Cass, it's three o'clock in the fucking morning. You can't wake me up and then tell me nothing is wrong.*"

I slid out of the bed trying not to disturb Log. My breath caught in my throat when he stopped snoring. I waited in silence, poised mid-step, worried that I had woken him and would have to come up with an excuse why I was out of bed. A minute felt like an eternity as I watched Logan roll onto his other side; his soft snores resuming almost instantaneously.

"I-I..." I stammered, shoving on some clothes, unsure what excuse I could come up with. Trying to create a believable lie. "I'm scared..." I murmured. The door creaked as I opened it, a small gap I could only just push through. I held my breath as I shut it behind me.

I tiptoed down the hallway, stopping when I reached the bedroom that had once been Jax's. "I know Cass, Logan told me about the nightmares." He replied, his voice gruff and ladened with exhaustion. "Logan has been going through defense plans. He is always creating new and more complex strategies to ensure yours and Felix's safety. Jax is never coming back here."

I nodded, trying to ignore the pang in my chest at the thought of never seeing Jax again. It was a pointless effort. Finding myself standing in front of his door, my hand on the brass doorknob. It refused to budge, but just when I was about to accept defeat, the mechanism suddenly clicked.

Looking over my shoulder, I snuck inside. It was clear no one had been in this room since before the War. A lump formed in the back of my throat. He *left, expecting to return.*

For over two years, the door had sealed in the scent of him. That alluring fragrance that drew me to him at the Masquerade Ball. My heart ached as the aroma grew stronger the deeper, I ventured into the room. Each breath felt like fire; every beat of my heart gave it more fuel. *I miss him.*

The room was dimly lit by the sliver of moonlight that filtered through the gap in the drapes. His bed basked in the silver glow. I ran my fingers across the dust-covered desk. *Why did Logan allow this room to be left like this? A shrine to his exiled brother. The same brother who wanted to steal everything from him?*

Notebooks and pens were still strewn across the surface beside unopened travel guides. A note sat on top of them. *Places Cassidy would love.* But there was one book that caught my attention—a black hardcover sketch pad.

I never knew Jax could draw, I thought as I gave into my compulsion to open it. Instantly regretting my decision when page upon page of images sketched in dark charcoal depicted intimate scenes of the two of us. Images of our bodies entwining in front of various landscapes. I recognized Verancas and Trikara almost instantly.

As I thumbed through the pages, the last drawing he had completed made my blood run cold. It was almost an identical scene to that of my nightmares; the details all intricately sketched in dark, angry strokes. It was an image of a hand clutching a human heart like an apple. Blood trickled down the wrist and through the fingers. Drawn with exquisite detail, I could almost feel the heart still throbbing its last few beats as I stared at the page. I could recognize that hand anywhere, with a faint mole below his thumb–Jax's.

I backed away from the sketchbook, tripping on strewn clothes and placing my hands out to stop me from falling. They clutched onto the bed while I stared for a few moments at the unmade bedding. The sheets were thrown back, looking as though he had only just left. It felt like he was due back at any moment. A chill ran along my spine as I sat at the foot of the bed. *Why am I here?*

The compulsion to feel close to him overwhelmed me as I lay back, my head sinking into his pillow. *Why do I miss him?*

"*Cass... I miss you too.*"

My eyes snapped open upon hearing Jax's voice, as loud and as clear as if he was in the room. Scanning the shadows, I felt like an idiot. *Of course, he isn't here.* My chest tightened as my disappointment kicked in. *I shouldn't want to see him. I shouldn't want him. At all.*

Tears filled my eyes as I fled the room; forcing Jax out of my mind as I silently maneuvered through the corridors. The oil paintings and tapestries were a blur as I passed them, yet there was one my eyes seemed drawn to that caused me to halt abruptly.

It was the lake - *my lake.* I was struck by the familiarity, the way the painter had captured its tranquility. It made me want to go there, to sit at the lake's edge and absorb the calming silence and stillness. *Why had I never noticed this before?* My eyes scrutinized every miniscule detail; picking out the differences between the painting and the lake as I knew it.

The towering evergreens that shrouded the lake were missing, instead replaced by luscious green fields. The fortified stone wall that divided Estoria from the rest of Eyre was also not there. In the painting, a large stag was drinking from the lake.

I staggered back a little when I noticed it - a face looking up at the stag from the watery depths, a woman. The longer I stared at it, the more faces emerged. I stifled a gasp, looking for the plaque beside it that would depict its origin like the others that hung beside it. But there was only a small, illegible squiggle for a signature.

Over a hundred times I have walked this corridor, yet I had never seen this painting before. *Has it recently been put there? If so, by whom?* This was 'The Lake of Lost Souls', as Elder Jeremiah referred to it. *My* lake.

I turned my back on it, trying to push aside the haunting image of the faces lurking in the tranquil water I was so fond of. I refused to let a painting disturb my happy moments of mine and Logan's sacred place. *I will get Logan to have it taken down.*

The lower corridors of the castle were deathly quiet, too. *Maybe I am still dreaming.* There were no guards following my every move, no cooks in the kitchen preparing breakfast. I pinched myself, hard. The pain was genuine as my nails bit into my flesh.

I opened the wooden door that led into the courtyard. Memories flooded back of sneaking out with Jax and taking Sophora from the stables. Riding out so we could watch the sunrise in Trikara. I felt a sharp pain in my chest. *Sophora.*

Her pen in the stables had remained empty ever since. I had not been down to the stables since her death. Losing her had hit me harder than I could have ever expected. *Another innocent life taken in the war because of my indecisiveness.* The crisp early morning air froze the air in my lungs, my shallow breaths became vapor before my eyes. It's icy-bite nipping at my nose and cheeks. I allowed the coolness to seep through my skin, chilling my bones and clearing my mind of all thoughts.

A loud caw startled me. A crow bigger than any I had seen before stood on the dewy lawn a few feet before me. Its beady black eyes stared directly at me as it stayed unnaturally still. Absentmindedly, I took a few steps towards it, almost as if it was compelling me to get closer.

A vision of chaos flashed through my mind the second my eyes connected with the crow's. Hundreds of armored men slashing at faceless creatures. Flooding the streets of Estoria, outnumbering the royal guards tenfold. In this vision, I watched them invade the castle, leaving a river of blood in their wake.

I yelped, tearing my eyes away from the crow. My peripheral vision caught a shadow dart out of sight elsewhere in the courtyard. An ominous feeling came over me, a sense that I should not be there. The crow cawed loudly as it took flight.

Suddenly, I felt alone - *vulnerable*. Turning on my heel, I noticed I had traveled further along the path from the castle than I had realized. So entranced by the crow and the vision that had taken over.

The hairs on the back of my neck stood on end as I took a brisk walk back to the castle, each step mimicking the pounding of my heartbeat in my ears. I felt like I was being watched. *I shouldn't be here. I should be with Logan where it's safe.*

I reached out for the handle and tugged at the door. It rattled on its hinges but refused to open. *How can it be locked?* I pummeled my fists on the doors frantically. A black mass inched closer until its shadow cast over me.

"Flynn!" I desperately called through our telepathic connection. But it was too late. A fog clouded my brain and blurred my vision. Paralysis seeped into every fiber of my body, I could feel myself falling, helpless to do anything to prevent it.

"Flynn... help... me."

ELEVEN

Eleanor was *furious*. I did not need to see the scowl on her face or the hatred in her eyes to feel her seething in anger. Her aura pulsed in rage, causing ripples of her energy to vibrate through the room.

"Please tell me you are not seriously considering Jax's proposal?" she hissed, her arms reaching out to me, spinning me around to face her instead of looking out of the window. "Babe, you know he is just *using* you... it's all he has ever done." Her voice softened as her fingers stroked my face, her eyes glassy.

"I have done *everything* you have asked me to do. I have tried to accept Jax. To understand your feelings for him. Hell, I have even tried to settle for just being your *plaything*. But... I refuse to stand by and watch you make the biggest mistake of your life."

Eleanor's eyes never left mine as she spoke. Her fingers traced spiral patterns against my neck, "I know you think you *love* him, but he will *never* love you. Babe, you know he has a *soulmate*. You know that everything he is doing now is to try to win her back, don't you?"

People of Verancas did not believe in soulmates. Instead, preferring to succumb to our carnal desires, accepting pleasure in every form. A monogamous relationship was a rarity here. We had our favorites, but never we never tied ourselves to one singular person. Though Jax had changed my perspective. *Maybe I had a soulmate too, but I had been too busy to notice them. Choosing to revel in orgasms with the many, than searching for true love with one.*

I averted my eyes to the floor, my words clogging the back of my throat. *I know, but I want him. I have always wanted him.* I remembered the first time I ever laid eyes on Jax. A little over five years ago, we were both in our late teens. Foolish and stupid.

I had been strolling across the beach; my eyes fixed on the sand that wedged between my toes with each step. Squelching with every step I took as I tried to work out how I was going to keep my secret from the world. A secret that would rock my entire existence should anyone find out. It had only been revealed to me a few days ago, my mother's words echoed in my mind as she took her final breaths. *"Your father is the devil... His darkness is inside of you."*

Tears blurred my eyes as I dragged my feet along the sand. *I wish I never knew who my father was. I already had one secret that was difficult to keep; now I had two.*

I failed to notice him at first. Only as I drew closer to the rock pools did I see the top of his dark blond head. It poked over the jagged, moss-covered rocks as he climbed from the other side. His piercing blue eyes glanced in my direction. My heart stopped beating.

"What?" he said, with a charming smirk on his face.

"You should be careful. Those rocks are slippery. Plus, the tide is coming in." I precariously strolled over to him, forcing myself to breathe and silently pleading with the butterflies in my stomach to cease their fluttering. *This boy is trouble.*

He shrugged and pressed forward. *He's fearless... no, careless.* I looked up at the base of the rock he was standing on.

"I know what I'm doing!" he chuckled.

Arrogant too. It was my turn to smirk. His accent gave him away. *He is not from around here. I would have noticed him here in Verancas. Perhaps he is from Svaalgard or Eyre.*

"You're a city boy..." I teased. "What do you know about climbing rocks?" I looked at his feet. "You're not even wearing the right shoes."

I continued to study his attire, a white shirt, beige pants and tan brogues. *Definitely not from around here.* My gaze diverted to my own clothes. Denim shorts that barely covered my butt cheeks and showcased my long, tanned legs. Paired with a red cropped t-shirt and a pair of flip-flops.

He was about to retort, descending the rocks as if they were stairs. When suddenly, an enormous wave crashed against the rock behind him; sweeping him off of his feet.

All I could do was watch in slow motion as he tumbled down the rock face, arms and legs flailing as he tried to stop himself. I rushed over to him when he finally came to a stop at the bottom. He had landed face first in an indistinguishable heap, groaning in pain as he slowly unfurled in the sand. The extent of his injuries were unknown, but from his torn shirt I could see every piece of exposed flesh was covered in abrasions from the jagged rocks. Somewhere along the way down he had lost a shoe, the other one barely made it, scuffed and mutilated beyond repair. My eyes raked over his limbs, searching for any signs of broken bones. I saw the bright red seep through his floppy blond locks as blood cascaded down his face.

"Shit..." I cussed, taking off my shirt and balling it up to stem the blood. He flinched, his blue eyes peering out of tiny slits. "I told you... but *nooo,* you city boys always know best," I muttered, lifting his hand away to assess his injury. Luckily, it was a minor cut, just above his eyebrow, but it looked deep. "I think it might need stitches."

His eyes focused on my cleavage in the red bikini top I wore beneath my top. The small triangles of fabric barely contained my full bosom. "I will be fine," he murmured, his hands wrapping behind my waist, pulling me down to straddle his lap. The knock to the head had not knocked his confidence. My hand stilled as his hot breath danced over my naked skin. "But if I don't live... I want to die happy."

"Babe—are you even listening?" Eleanor snapped her fingers in front of my face. Her voice held a coldness to it that was not there before. She was no longer touching me; instead, her arms were folded across her chest.

"Is this how it is going to be? You are actually going to choose *him* over *me?"* she sighed, not meeting my gaze. "After everything I have done to *protect* your *secrets...*"

I let her words sink in. I was a wounded when Eleanor first found me. Determined to handle my shapeshifting curse on my own. *I did not need anyone, certainly not my father's guidance.* As soon as I had turned eighteen, my 'spirit' animal had awakened. A raven with feathers as dark as night. Xeyiera's history has not been kind to shifters, feared like werewolves and witches. Humans feared the magic in our DNA that allowed our bodies to go beyond what was physically possible and the animalistic instincts ingrained in our souls. *It was a curse.*

Recalling the first time I had taken to the sky during the day, the day Eleanor found me, I winced; feeling the injuries of my inexperience. I was not used to the vibrant colors and bright lights of my bird's vision; so much more intricate and complex. The world was so radiant and vivid; the flowers in bloom were in colours naked to the human eye. The grass was so much greener and the sky become a vast spectrum of blues; even the sun's aura glowed a magnitude of ambers and golds as I soared beneath it. It was jarring, like seeing the world through a kaleidoscope.

As soon as I had taken flight, instant regret had set in. Blinded and disorientated, I collided with a branch of a tree, landing on the ground with a deafening thud. Bones shattered upon impact. My left wing throbbed and was crooked at an unnatural angle. The pain was so intense; I thought I was going to die.

A pair of hands scooped me up, her dark eyes peering down at me with a kind smile on her face. "It's okay, fledgling. I will look after you." Eleanor had taken me to her home, wrapping me in a blanket. I panicked, thinking if I became human, the pain would be tolerable.

I had expected Eleanor to be shocked to find a young, naked woman writhing in pain on her dining room floor. Clutching at my arm, screaming in agony. But Eleanor was the opposite. She coaxed me to her couch, her voice as gentle as her touch.

"I am like you," she whispered to me, bandaging my severely broken arm into a sling. "I have been watching you. I am honor-bound to protect *our* species and it is my duty to help fledglings like yourself. The moment I saw your sporadic flight path, your unnatural actions in bird form, I knew I had to help you." She sighed. "Though I had hoped not under these circumstances."

Eleanor cared for me until I recovered from my injury. During those weeks, we had become close, teaching me all there was to know about the history of our kind. Helping me control my shifting between forms and how to mimic the actions of a real bird. It did not take long for our relationship to take a different turn.

While people of Verancas loved and fucked freely, I had never been with a woman before Alyiah. She helped me explore my sexuality; opening my eyes to pleasure I had never experienced before. Together we developed a deeper connection, somewhat similar to the one I had with Jax. More than just lust; as close to love as I would ever get. Everything I knew I owed to her.

My eyes swept over the only person who had ever shown me any genuine care and affection. *Can I really turn my back on her?*

"Lena..." I sighed, reaching out for her. "I don't have a choice." I hoped she could see the sincerity in my eyes. She relaxed her arms, allowing my fingers to intertwine with hers. "You saw him after the war... wounded, scared... *broken*... he needs *our* help... like I needed yours."

A sudden rush of warmth flooded through my body as she kissed me. Her tongue parted my lips to deepen the kiss, her hands intertwined with mine.

"I love you. It- it hurts to see you with *him*." She turned her head away as a tear rolled down her cheek. "I thought what we had was mutual, but I can see it in your eyes; he will always come before me. I can't be second best. I refuse to watch him ruin your life."

"Lena..." I begged, trying to stop her from walking out of the door. "I... I..." The word love choked me. We had never said this to one another before; chartering a new territory. Realizing I was just as inexperienced about love as I was at being a shifter.

"I love you too... but if you truly loved me, you would want me to be happy... and you *both* make me happy... Please don't make me choose between you and Jax."

Eleanor stiffened. I knew I had crossed a line. I should let her walk out of my life, knowing I would inflict nothing but heartbreak and pain. But my selfish and possessive beast would not relinquish the hold I had over her. Refusing to let go of the pleasure she gave me and the stability I needed. Nor would it give up on the dream of sitting beside Jax on the throne of Estoria.

I drew her closer to me, my hands wandering beneath the waistline of her jeans, brushing her warmth with my fingertips. "Lena... I will always need you..." I murmured, teasing her wet slit with one of my fingers before slipping in a second. Instinctively her hips began to gyrate. "I will always want you... I will *always* love you."

I felt her resolve slip as I dragged her to the bed, laying her down and sliding off her jeans. I drew her into my arms, planting a passionate kiss on her lips. I never gave her a chance to argue; to deny me of her body. as I showered her gorgeous body with urgent, passionate kisses.

"Let me *show* you how much you mean to me... Let me prove to you how much I *want* you."

TWELVE

A pair of pale blue eyes looked up at me, but they did not see me. His head of floppy dark hair was now matted and sticky. Stooping down to his level, I realized he was gone; that despite focusing all my attention on trying to heal him, I had failed. My heart broke knowing that my first and only child was dead. The fire he possessed snuffed out before he could reach his full potential.

Through glassy eyes, I memorized every line of his face, imprinting them forever in my mind and my heart. I would never see him smile, never hear him laugh, never watch him grow into the man he was destined to be–King of Eyre. He will be nothing but a footnote in the history of the Kingdom. Long forgotten, like the other bones in the castle's catacomb. It brought me a small comfort to know my baby would not be completely alone in the cold crypt for all eternity.

Yet there was no real comfort for a grieving mother. Especially to one whose child had been so barbarically slaughtered by his uncle. I lifted my hands to my face, sickened as the liquid crimson trickled down my arms as I prayed. Prayed for the Gods to bring him back to me, but my prayers went unanswered.

"Find the King... I want his head on a spike at the main gate by sunrise... an example to all who dare rise against me." The familiar voice was distant, muffled due to the thick stone walls that separated us–Jax. I blocked my thoughts in a desperate attempt to shield myself from him. The door swung open with a loud crash. It was too late. He found me.

"I warned you. You should have chosen me."

I screamed. Sitting bolt upright, gasping for breath, while my hands clutched the duvet to my chest. Beads of ice-cold sweat clung to my forehead and trickled down my spine. Before I could stop the tears, my sobs erupted from my chest, wracking my body until the bed shook along with it.

"Cass..." Logan cooed; his face contorted with worry as he sat up and enveloped me in his warm embrace. My words clogged my throat, my breath frozen in my lungs. "*That* will never happen." Logan said, trying to comfort me, but the tremor he tried to hide in his voice was less convincing. There was a cold brush of his metallic limb against my cheek as he tried to wipe away the tears that streaked my face. "I promise you, Cass... *nothing* will harm either of you." I sniffed in response, burying my face into his chest, the image of the limp corpse of my child still tormenting me.

"Cass, he will never get through the gates..." Logan paused, tilting my chin up towards him, his lips gently fluttered over mine. I watched as he slowly let go of me and flung back the duvet from his naked body. My eyes followed his firm buttocks. Listening to the soft padding of his footsteps as he tiptoed across the room. Stopping every few steps to retrieve his clothing that we discarded in haste the night before. "I don't think any of the kitchen staff is up yet... but I will rustle up something to eat."

My faint smile in the darkness went unnoticed, but my thoughts had not strayed far from my dream. The hole carved in my son's chest, his blank open eyes and face of pure terror and anguish. My stomach churned as nausea set in and bile rose in the back of my throat.

"I'm not hungry..." I whispered. "but... I think I might check on Felix-" Logan saw the hesitation in my eyes, and heard my anxious thoughts of entering my son's room. He leaned over me, his lips delicately brushed my forehead.

"Cass, it *was* just a nightmare, but I will bring Felix here if that would help ease your mind?" I nodded, watching Logan slip out of the room. Darkness washed over me the moment the door shut behind him, leaving me alone with nothing but my thoughts for company. The silence that befell the room was heavy and ominous. Completely different to the silence I sought when visiting the lake.

"*I will take back what is mine, Cassidy.*" Jax's voice vibrated in my skull. "*Whatever the cost.*"

A flurry of loud squawks and the frantic beating of wings startled me and drowned out the rest of Jax's sentence. I grabbed the robe draped upon the chair beside the bed. Pulling it around me hastily as I rushed to the window. I threw open the curtain, my eyes blinded by the sudden brightness of the hazy morning sun. It took a few moments for my vision to adjust, making out the outline of an enormous black bird. *How can this one bird cause such a commotion?*

As dark as night, a crow perched on the stone window ledge. It preened its glossy feathers, revealing an iridescent, oily sheen. They shimmered with streaks of magenta, emerald and sapphire as the sun rays reflected off of them. I watched as it bobbed closer to the window, using its black beak to tap on the glass. Its beady black eyes stared at me as if trying to reach into my soul.

How strange, I thought, opening the window in a trance, the crow's unblinking eyes locked onto mine. *What could you possibly want in here?*

The crow stepped through the gap, bringing with it a strange sense of familiarity. *Are you the bird I see in my dreams?*

Its silky feathers glided against my hand, sending a ripple of electricity through it. A chorus of whispers filled my ears before my mind exploded with vivid colors and shapes, none of which were distinguishable. I tried to focus, to pick out a specific voice or to make sense of the images that whirred, to no avail.

Stretching out my hand, I gently placed it on the bird's back. I could feel the vibration of its heart beating frantically. *It's ok little crow,* I thought, allowing my fingers to stroke its soft, shiny feathers. *I'm not going to harm you.*

"*But someone wants to harm you.*" A voice whispered in my mind. "*He is coming... and so is death.*"

Startled, I snatched my hand away from the bird. I shook my head as I began backing away from the window. *I'm still dreaming... this isn't real.*

"*Cassidy... trust me.*" The voice said once more, its internal voice now frantic. "*I have been trying to warn you-*" The sound of the heavy door opening made the crow jump. "*I was hoping you all would have fled...*" It panicked, unfurling its wings as it scurried back outside onto the window ledge. "*I shouldn't have come...*" It continued to mutter, yet its feet still remained rooted to the stone ledge. "*But I needed to warn you... one last time...*"

In a flurry of black, the crow was gone. I watched until all that had become of it was a small black speck against the amber haze of the morning sunrise. Once it had disappeared, I spun around to face two pairs of brown eyes staring at me.

"There is mama!" Logan's voice cooed, carrying Felix in his arms. The amber glow of the morning sun made dark shadows flicker over his face. "But why is she out of bed?" he asked, keeping his voice light but his words were laden with concern.

I sighed, allowing my feet to guide me to them. Unable to tear my eyes away for a moment, reaching out to touch them; to make sure they were both real.

Felix was Logan's double; from his shock of dark hair to the exact shade of brown of his eyes. It reminded me of velvety chocolate, Felix's favorite treat. His chubby, round face bore dimples as he smiled. My fingertips brushed against his soft cheeks. The vice-tight grip that held my chest captive was released. *I have never been so relieved.*

I wrapped my arms around them both. Taking long, deep breaths to steady my frantic heartbeat, and inhaling their scents as I reveled in the heat that radiated from their bodies. I buried my head in Felix's hair to hide the tears spilling down my cheeks. The scent of lavender clung to his skin from his bedtime bath. Its aroma soothed my worries and pushed back the horrific scenes from my dream. Planting a kiss on the top of his head, I felt Logan's hot breath against my ear.

"I love you. I may be King, but you and Felix will always be my priority," he said as he planted a kiss on my cheek. His other hand tucked a loose curl behind my ear. "Until my last breath, I will fight to protect you both. You have my word."

THIRTEEN

Three days before Cassidy's disappearance
Logan

I smiled at the sight of my two most important people in the world softly snoring beside me, my arm stretched over them like a protective shield. *I will protect them at all costs.* Yet the blinding glare of the sunlight danced on my iron limb, a harsh reminder of my weakness. *But what if I fail them?*

Every night for the past month, Cassidy had been suffering with night-terrors. One that sparked her worst fear: that I would die at the hands of my brother.

It was jarring to see them replay in her thoughts as she woke screaming and sobbing; watching Jax brutally tear apart our perfect family with his ruthless passion as he sought revenge. I knew he was out there, still clutching at straws in the hope that he could reclaim what he believes should be his - praying that Cassidy would one day change her mind. Jax's anger and hatred forged a path that took him beyond redemption; manifesting as this evil being in her dreams was in fact pushing her away. Her vivid dreams, so believable and lifelike, scared me, but they also drove a bigger wedge between them; Cassidy was less likely to change her mind if she feared he would harm her child.

I had not yet told Cassidy of the grizzly crimes Jax had already committed. Even though she had a right to know, I was not prepared to make her nightmares worse. Instead, I focused my efforts on making the castle impenetrable; trying to ignore my inner voice that told me I was weak for this clunky chunk of metal that prevented me from wielding a sword. *All I can do now is trust in my Royal Guard.*

Yet, I knew that would not be enough. I had made allies with the neighboring King-doms to strengthen our borders; I also had the Elders on my side... for the most part. A select few did not agree with the changes I had made, but they were outnumbered. As long as Elder Jeremiah believed in me, they all had to abide by my reign without question. Though I was hesitant to include them in my plans. *They could not see me as a weak king that fell at the first hurdle.*

My eyes scanned over Cassidy's face. Watching her sleep blissfully, her beauty radiating even in the darkness. My soulmate. I owed her more than I could ever give her in return; I owed her my life and I will fight to the death to protect her. I will never back down.

A shiver shot down my spine as I thought about Cassidy's choice. *What if she hadn't picked me? I'd be dead and Jax would be here in my place.* I had preparations and strategies to discuss, plans I needed to make. *I will not let Jax take everything from me.*

I was heading towards the Map Room, ready to study every square inch of the kingdom for weak spots or points of interest that Jax may use against me. Though I found myself wandering the fortified walls of the castle, my gaze was on the healing Kingdom of Eyre.

The morning sky romanticized the scene before me, casting everything it touched in its amber hue. Obscuring the battle scars that had been permanently etched across the land. From the now grassy craters in the field, reminders of where the trolls had fallen, to the dilapidated buildings caused by the riots that broke out before and after the War. The fractions within the Kingdom were slowly disappearing, so that the kingdom could be as one. Only time could ease the survivors' wounds and allow them to forgive one another.

Though the majority of the people were loyal to me, I knew there were some who secretly wished for my demise. Those who would not think twice to follow Jax, should he challenge my position.

As I pushed in my search for a better vantage point, I headed towards the north-west turret. Jax's threat whispered in the wind. "*You will be the one who dies. I will not hesitate. Nor will I hesitate to plunge a blade through the heart of your child, should she bear one.*"

The sting of betrayal seeped into my mind as my eyes scanned the awakening kingdom below. Guards stood vigil in their positions or marched through the streets while the people of Estoria began their day. I knew Cassidy could not help the connection that bound her and Jax. But knowing she was still in contact with him ate away at my insides. I found myself keeping her at an arm's length. *I can't take the risk of Jax having direct access to such knowledge.*

I knew she hated the entourage of guards following her, hated being cooped up in the castle. *But until Jax was gone, what else could I do to protect her?* In a twisted way, I started to enjoy her fear. A part of me I never knew existed had been awakened at the sight of her being petrified when she woke from her dreams. It appeased my insecurities, seeing her strong reaction to this dream; it confirmed that she also wanted what I wanted–to remain at my side.

She chose me, despite being on the brink of death, despite being grievously injured. She took the risk of choosing me, knowing that I may not have made it to the following morning. Yet I was still tormented by their connection; wondering what lies Jax was feeding her without my knowledge. Unable to do anything about the feelings she tried to deny she had for him. Until one of us was dead, they would be forever intertwined and I would be riddled with doubt.

On the battlefield, I struggled to envision the death of my brother. Unable to attack, only withstand his onslaught of blows. Even now, I struggled to envision a world where I would have to kill him. *But I have no choice. He wants to take Cassidy. He will murder my infant son in cold blood.*

My gaze flitted across the boroughs that bordered either side of the fortified entrance; Faelfoy and Winro. Carbon-copy houses sat in neat identical rows. Their gardens pruned to perfection much mimicking the borough closest to the castle of Ralco. Even those pristine streets had not been immune to the riots that had ricocheted from tavern to tavern. Remembering it as though it only happened yesterday. Fists flying through the air, the shattering of glass, and the staccato beat of footsteps as the angry mobs tore through the boroughs.

Fic, the industrial borough, was functioning once more; fulfilling orders from across the lands. Cassidy's father's blacksmiths were already churning out more weaponry. I had been both impressed and horrified by the alarming rate they had produced the artillery and ammo to equip both sides of the War. The place would be a target for destruction, should Jax invade so I had placed extra patrols around its perimeter to ensure its safety.

My eyes strayed to Thamesleep; the agricultural hub for Estoria. After fortifying our walls, my father, when he was king, wanted Estoria to be completely independent. The borough grew crops of vegetables and fruit, as well as grains and wheat. Some even reared livestock for meat. They flourished under his reign, providing plenty during the summer to store for the winter months; even selling surplus beyond the walls of Estoria and the kingdom of Eyre. Yet as a result of the war, many farms struggled to recover as most of the farmers and their sons had been killed or fatally wounded in the battle.

I sighed as I watched the tractors plow the fields. Most of the farmers were widows or children who should be at school. For the first time in a long time, we relied on imported food to survive. *Would Jax use this to his advantage?*

As my eyes glanced across to the western part of the borough, they lingered on the most recent construction; a cemetery. The resting place for the fallen soldiers. Over three thousand people had lost their lives that day, and another one thousand suffered from life-changing injuries—myself included.

I averted my eyes to my makeshift hand as a surge of anger coursed through me, flowing like molten lava through my veins. I had always been the better fighter, and he knew by taking that hand, he would forever put me at a disadvantage.

While the Royal Guard had strict instructions—protect the Queen and Prince at all costs, I could not help but pray he would not come any time soon.

But he will come, the voice inside my head told me.

FOURTEEN

Nineteen Months Ago
Jax

I knew exactly where Alyiah was. Not that I was happy about it. Knowing she was keeping her former girlfriend's bed warm. *But who am I to complain? It's not like my bed is empty.*

In fact, unless Alyiah was around, I would find a girl, *any* girl, to spend the night with. Someone who I could use to take my mind away from Cassidy; from feeling every intimate detail between her and *Logan*. I had thought that with Cassidy's pregnancy, their sex life would slow down and become stale. *Manageable.* But I was wrong; if anything, it had become worse: more frequent, more passionate.

Cassidy's pregnancy had unlocked something within me. A monster born of undeniable jealousy that spiraled into uncontrollable rage. In these moments, I would fuck rough and hard. *Brutal* to the point of physically hurting these girls. Some were into it, too full of lust to register the pain, while others despised me for it.

The blonde before me was on all fours, her slit glistening, waiting for me to enter. But I had another idea. I grasped a handful of her hair, pulling hard as I slid my member deep into her dry, tight ass. She squealed like a wounded animal while tears sprung from her eyes.

"Stop!" she sobbed, "Please... stop!"

I ignored her, too overwhelmed in my determination to push Cassidy's emotions aside. Desperately trying not to feel her happiness and her pleasure. Being her soulmate was torture; she was the first thing I thought about when I woke up and the last thing before

I succumbed to sleep, and every moment in between. Everything reminded me of her. I missed not seeing her, being near her. *"I will get you back, Cassidy. You are mine."*

I continued thrusting into this girl's rosebud, imagining it was Cassidy. Replacing the girl's cries with Cassidy's soft purrs. Each imagined moan took me closer to my release. My nails dug into the girl's hips. She hissed, trying to free herself from my grip, but I held on tighter. My muscles stiffening as I shot my load deep into her, enjoying each ripple of pleasure that pulsated through me. When I finally pulled my cock out of her, I watched as my cum spilled from her gaping ass.

The girl wasted no time, scrambling off of the bed and snatching up her items of clothing on the floor. Trying to stifle her sobs as she pulled on each one, wincing as she pulled up her pants. I smirked with satisfaction. It did not go unnoticed. Her hand flew through the air, landing on my cheek with a resounding smack.

I did not flinch. My eyes narrowed into slits as I rubbed my right cheek, feeling the skin burn from her contact. "Is that all you got?" I shrugged, getting to my own feet, drawing up in front of her at my full height. I towered over her.

A fat tear rolled down her cheek. "Fuck you, Jax," she hissed, storming out of the room.

"You already have..." I muttered in response, allowing myself to crash back down on the bed, relieved that Cassidy and Logan had finally gone to sleep.

I allowed myself to fall into a light slumber, my thoughts still on Cassidy. *Why had I asked Alyiah to marry me?* I asked myself, *when I have no intentions of replacing Cassidy? To make her jealous? Out of spite?*

No, I needed Alyiah. More like I needed something *from* her—her continued cooperation. I needed her to have a reason to want to find her father quicker, to get Demi's resurrection completed. *The sooner I build my army, the less time I have to wait to get Cassidy back.*

I knew Ayliah had feelings for me. That was my leverage; the easiest way I could get her to do what I wanted. As long as I played my part well, I would have my chance to reclaim everything that is owed to me.

The proposal was designed to make Cassidy jealous, seeing how far I could push her before she admitted her feelings for me. Despite her desperate attempts to conceal her thoughts, I could read Cassidy like a book. She hated me being with someone else; *especially* Alyiah. It still brought a smile to my face when I recalled her envious face and angry thoughts the first time they met. I often fantasized of that night, the four of us in Alyiah's hut. Watching the two of them pleasuring Cassidy, enjoying the innocent look fade from her eyes as she allowed them to bring her to climax. I did not mind sharing her, but not with *him,* my brother. *She is my soulmate. Cassidy belongs to me.*

I sighed, glaring up at the yellowing ceiling of the room I currently called home. The lumpy mattress beneath dug into my kidneys and spine; a stark contrast to the luxurious room I took for granted in the castle; with a huge four-poster oak bed. The floral wallpaper was peeling in parts, or stained with black mold in others. It was obvious from the outside, with crumbling stone walls and broken shutters on the windows, that this place would be awful inside. Yet, I had no choice, stumbling here after my humiliating defeat. The only place in Verancas that never asked for ID. *Beggars could not be choosers.*

My thoughts drifted from that humiliating night back to Alyiah. Particularly my discovery of who her father was. None other than *the* most feared being in all of Xeyiera: the necromancer known as the Phantom. She had told me in a moment of vulnerability. Sharing her fear of the darkness that was inside her during a drunken night we spent together. I doubted she even remembered she had told me. *But I will never forget.*

After that night, I visited her at least once a month. Naïve in my hope that she would be a capable distraction in the absence of my soulmate; that I could grow to love her as she loved me, or that I could live without the person I was predestined to be with.

Alyiah was always so happy, vibrant, and carefree. Life in Verancas was so different than it was in Eyre. The kingdom had little to no rules, ever since the Elders relinquished their hold. They felt no pressure to find a soulmate, rejecting the very idea. Free to fuck a partner, or multiple, finding pleasure for the sake of pleasure; choosing who they loved. I had wanted to escape my brother's shadow and leave Estoria once Logan took the throne after my father. But my plans changed the moment my father gave me the hope that I could become King, and even more so the moment I laid eyes on Cassidy.

The thought of Cassidy tucked up in my brother's bed, sleeping blissfully in his arms, filled me with pure, unadulterated rage. *I* deserved that happiness, too. *I* deserved to get *my* happily ever after. Yet, as long as Logan still breathed, I would never get it.

I cursed myself for my lapse in judgement during the battle; for allowing myself to become overwhelmed by the sentimentality of brotherhood. Letting emotions and memories cloud my perception, forgetting what mattered most: my soulmate. *My happiness.*

That was why I needed the necromancer. There was only one person who had always been on my side; who was demanding and ruthless. My twin–Demi. I could not envision a world where she did not exist. She had an energy about her that seemed to manifest all that she desired. Demi would know exactly what to do.

Ayliah avoided her father, constantly delaying taking me to him. Using her curvaceous body and seductive charm to distract me from my cause. But no more. The promise of marrying her, of making her my Queen, would give her an incentive to please me; *to do exactly as I want to be happy.*

My eyes finally flickered closed. My fists scrunched up into tight balls as I fought back the rage that was threatening to consume me once more. I focused on steadying my breaths, trying to match hers. Momentarily, I imagined her beside me. *I will take back what is mine.*

FIFTEEN

Cassidy

Blood. Lots of it. Rivulets winding through the gaps in the stone floor, forming pools beneath my feet. Sprays of it splattered the walls, slowly trickling down the walls. It was a bloodbath. The scene before me belonged to a massacre, but all of this blood came from one person. My husband: Logan.

What was left of his lifeless body lay in the middle of the room. His dismembered limbs were scattered around him; his head was unaccounted for.

I stepped closer. My brain could not process the sight of his mangled corpse; unable to comprehend the brutal way his life had ended. A barbaric and brutal act of cold-blooded murder. Far too inhuman for a man. Yet, there Jax stood, holding his brother's head like a trophy. His sword was still slick with blood, as were his clothes. But it was his face that chilled me to the core. A pair of bright blue eyes clashing with the crimson that speckled his face. A sinister grin twisted on his lips from beneath his beard.

Jax's gaze locked onto me, his eyes sparkling with smug, deranged delight. Proud of the carnage he has caused.

"I told you Cassidy, you are mine."

A bright light startled me from the vision. The impenetrable darkness dissolving as my eyes slowly opened. *Where the fuck am I?*

I tried to scream, but nothing more than a strangled whimper escaped my lips. Sharp stabbing pains shot through my body as I tried to sit up, my head heavy and thick, as if struggling with a hangover. *What the fuck?*

My heart hammered in my chest. Beads of cold sweat ran down my spine and goosebumps pricked my skin. An ear-splitting scream reverberated throughout the room. It took a moment to realize who was screaming: *me.*

From out of nowhere, a hand clamped over my mouth. The aroma of cedar wood and smoke permeated their flesh. *What the fuck is going on? Who the fuck is this?*

The walls were lined with thick wooden shelves. They were cluttered with books, dusty potion bottles, and unidentifiable objects. As my vision cleared, I spotted several large glass jars. Each one held something gruesome and macabre. A severed finger, an eyeball and a human fetus suspended in formaldehyde, to name a few.

"I am going to remove my hand, but don't *scream.*" A male voice whispered in my ear. "If you do, we are *both* dead."

Tentatively, the pressure over my mouth eased. Though my kidnapper remained close, moving into my view, his face inches from mine. Light hazel eyes peered into my own. I remained silent, watching as he slowly backed away. Perching himself on the chair opposite me, reminding me of a bird, ready to take flight. *Is he a-*

"Shapeshifter?" he responded, his bearded mouth pulled at the corners into a small smile. "Yes...but only because I am a mage."

Staring at him with a mix of awe as he manifested a single black feather in his palm, I tried to recall why he looked so familiar, but could not place where I knew him from. The feather suddenly burst into flame, leaving nothing but a small pile of ash in his hand. *Have I met him before?*

My thoughts went back to a few days ago. The crow that I had allowed in through the window feeling that same sense of familiarity. *But I have never met a mage before.* They always kept their identities a secret, preferring to dwell in the shadows elsewhere in Xeyiera. History had proven unkind time and time again to those who possessed ancient magic.

I watched as she brushed the ash from his hands, his shirt sleeve rising to reveal a tattoo on his forearm. Like the cattle in the fields of Thamesleep, he had been branded. The coat of arms inked onto his skin was instantly recognizable even in the dim candle-lit room. That was the purpose of them—to be easily identified as a member of the monarch's personal security detail. *He is, or at least was at some point, part of the Royal Guard.*

The tattoo symbolized their loyalty to the reign of their king. Each monarch had their own. I had helped Logan with his design not that long ago. Similar to his father's before him, both had a silver shield with two swords crossed behind it and thorny vines wrapped around. Dragon wings emerged from both sides, its head resting on top of the shield.

That was how I knew this coat of arms belonged to the Silverthorne legacy. Logan's great-great-great-grandfather had been the one to slay the last dragon that plagued Xeyiera. Their coat of arms represents that victorious moment. Logan's dragon was green, bearing its razor-sharp teeth, unlike the purple, sleeping dragon of his father's. I recalled the arm of Esan, Logan's most trusted guard. Showing off his new tattoo like trophies the day he had gotten it; both of them sitting side by side. The cogs slowly churned in my mind, *whoever he is, he is no longer part of the castle's protection detail.*

"You are one of Jax's men."

"I *was...*" he muttered, his gaze averting to the floor as he pulled out a small switch-blade from his pocket. He whittled away at the wooden arm of the chair, looking uncomfortable and full of remorse.

Questions dizzied my mind. *Why am I here? Why didn't he take me straight to Jax? What does he want with me?* Yet, I asked: "What is your name?"

The question seemed to catch him off guard. The pocket knife slipped and sliced into his thumb. He cursed, shoving it into his mouth, wincing at the pain. He mumbled something, but I could not hear him as he sucked on his wound. I shook my head to show I did not understand him. He repeated his words, but they were muffled and too quiet to comprehend.

"I didn't catch that."

"TOR-VUS!" He enunciated with an exasperated look, wiping his thumb in the leg of his pants. "My name is *Torvus.*"

"What do you want with me, Torvus?" I asked, shifting my feet from the couch to the floor as pins and needles crept up my legs.

His gaze snapped up to me, his eyes shining like beacons. "I tried to warn you, tried convincing you to leave..." his tone softened, becoming more somber, "before it was too late."

"You're the crow I keep seeing, aren't you? Are you *making* me have these night-mares?"

Torvus solemnly shook his head, his shoulders slumped, and his eyes, full of sorrow and remorse, locked onto mine. "Cassidy, those aren't dreams you're seeing..." he paused, flipping the pocket knife closed and slipping it back into the pocket of his filthy, tattered jeans. "They are *premonitions of the future...*"

No, no, no, no! Torvus' lips continued to move, but my heartbeat throbbed in my ears, drowning out the rest of his words. I got to my feet, shaking my head. The room was spinning, throwing me off balance. Suddenly feeling nauseous, aware that I could no longer feel the ground beneath my feet. Toppling forwards, my hands reached out to grab hold of something, *anything*, to stop myself from crashing to the floor on my face. *A stone floor is not a soft landing.*

My fingers sank into something soft, *flesh*, digging in my nails as I tried to use whatever it was for support. My vision was blurred by white-hot tears.

There was a sharp intake of breath. Blinking hard, I realized I was clutching onto Torvus' brawny arms, his muscular chest inches from my face. I could feel the sobs building in my chest, squeezing the air from my lungs as my tears spilled. Each one scorched my cheeks as they rolled down my face. I shook my head again as he drew me closer to him.

"I'm sorry, Cass..." he murmured. "but I know how it feels. Watching someone you love perish before your eyes..." His words caught in his throat, choking out the last few. "...At the hands of *Jax*."

SIXTEEN

Flynn

She has to be here somewhere! My hope of finding her curled up sleeping elsewhere in the castle diminished as we ran out of rooms to search. My eyes scanned the corridor, recalling the first time I had ever walked these halls during the Masquerade of Whispers: the night that changed everything.

The music was blaring; the bass throbbed through my chest and vibrated against my skull. It was almost unbearable: the thrum of feet pounding against the wooden floor as people danced, the babble of chatter hung in the air, mind-numbing and boring. I squirmed in my suit at the itchiness of thre starch. The mask I wore over my face slowly suffocated me and hindered my vision.

A beautiful girl in a red dress sauntered over to me. Long, white-blonde hair cascaded over her shoulders and rested on her breasts. The deep crimson gown clinging to her porcelain skin accentuated her cleavage. She gathered attention like metal shards to a magnet. All eyes glued to her as she continued to walk unabashedly with a small smile fixed on her lips. The girl looked as though she was completely oblivious to the eyes that followed the sway of her hips or she did not care.

"Hi, I'm Demi," she said, though her lips did not move. *"I know you can hear me."* Her eyes twinkled mischievously as she drew closer. *"And I know your secret."* Demi looked over her shoulder, her gaze focusing on the one person I had been avoiding all night. Forcing myself to focus solely on Cassidy and not look in his direction. *Jace.*

My palms felt sweaty. I shrugged, trying to remain nonchalant. *I knew coming here was a bad idea;* I thought. *I am a dead man.* Demi's lips parted as she laughed lightly, placing a hand on my shoulder.

"Your secret is safe with me..." She smiled. *"You should go speak to him. There is nothing suspicious about two men talking at a party!"*

Problem was, Jace and I were incapable of *just* talking. That was how we ended up getting hot and heavy, almost going too far, in this closet I was now desperately searching. *I need to find Cassidy.*

It was thanks to her, and King Logan, that we never needed to live in fear again. Demolishing Clause 4a meant loving someone of the same sex was no longer a punishable crime. *Cassidy made the right choice.*

Despite this, our love still carries a stigma. Prejudice will always prevail by those who supported the regime. *The Rules of Conduct.* These people still believed it was unnatural. *Immoral, disgusting, unnatural.* I could not blame them. Since a young age, the Rules of Conduct had been so indoctrinated that they refused to accept change; even I struggled to accept it at first. I had even used those very words to describe my feelings towards Jace–but he was my soulmate. *He made me feel whole.*

During The Masquerade, we had been so close to consummating our bond. Not caring how hurried and rushed it was; we were too desperate in our love and our *lust.* Nothing else mattered. Unable to think of anything else other than solidifying the bond. Our connection grew stronger as each day passed, making it harder to resist. At least, that was until Cassidy interrupted, thinking I was in trouble. *Now she is the one in trouble.*

I tried again to reach her through our telepathic link; shouting to her through the void repeatedly, being met by a resounding silence. Her mind was well and truly blocked. Typically, when she shields her mind from me, I could push through the barricade with a bit of persuasion and persistence. But not this time. The boundaries were impenetrable, not just to me, but to Logan as well.

Turning my back on the closest, cursing as my hand slammed it shut mid-turn. *Where the fuck is she? Why was she out of bed wandering around at two o-fucking-clock? How did she sneak past the guards? The castle should be teeming with them, let alone positioned outside of their bedroom. So where the fuck were they?*

A thought crossed my mind; but I refused to acknowledge it. Letting it niggle away at me as I made my way to the map room to speak to Logan. *Why weren't the guards in their appointed positions?*

A lump formed in my throat. It should be me on watch, but I had swapped as a one-off because it was Jace's birthday: the big three-oh. I had made plans to surprise him; a romantic meal and a *very* early night.

Cassidy had been trying to tell me something; something she felt was important. *She would not have woken me up in the morning if it wasn't.* Yet she had blocked her thoughts from me almost and decided against telling me. *What was she hiding? What did she want to say to me?*

I threw open the door to the map room, expecting Logan's dark eyes bearing into mine questioningly. Expecting him to demand why we, the Royal Guard, have not found the Queen. Yet the map room was eerily quiet, the chair he was often found sitting in, empty.

For the past two years, if he had not been with Cassidy and Felix, you would have found Logan here; hunched over a map or thumbing through yet another book. Too absorbed in his thoughts to notice anything or anyone else. The only time he was elsewhere in the castle was when he had visitors; rulers of the other kingdoms or the Elders. These appointments often took place in the throne room, the grandest and most prestigious place in the castle.

I stole a quick glance at the map stretched out across the table. Each corner was held down by a thick, leather-bound book. Dates and annotations were scribbled in the margins: sightings of Jax since the War, names of people who have confirmed his whereabouts, places he frequented, as well as any suspicious activity. Logan had been meticulous in his efforts. I had not seen this map before. A new one that bore small tears in the fold lines. *Why would Logan keep this map a secret?*

My eyes raked across the many notes. Jax had been in many suspicious places; The Prurient Nymph, Amorous Fox, Lucious Succubus and The Shapely Wench. They were all taverns by day and whore-houses by night.

Each place had its own symbol on the map, spanning from one side of Xeyiera to the other. *Why would Jax go to these whore houses?* Jax was handsome. With his dark blond hair, piercing blue eyes, and charming smile, he could dazzle any woman he wanted into bed. *Though the only woman he wants, did not want him.*

My gaze finally stopped on a new annotation. The ink was still wet, the rushed scrawl still bleeding into the parchment - yesterday's date. The symbol on the map showed it was in the northern part of Lythenyal; an infamous port for pirates. Supposedly, this was also a place for witches, mages, and other shady characters to gather. A perfectly secluded spot away from prying eyes.

"Flynn?" The sound of his voice startled me, knocking over the inkwell and spilling onto the map. *Shit!* I snatched the map up from the desk, but the damage was already done. Watching in horror as the black spread its way across the map and dripped from the bottom onto the floor.

"*Fuck*... your majesty... I-"

"Flynn it's ok." He sighed, his attention no longer focused on me. Logan shifted his son in one arm while trying to retrieve something out of his pocket with the other. Felix was squirming and crying at the top of his lungs, but Logan remained calm and collected. He pulled out an old rag and offered it to me, his eyes gesturing to the table that was now flooded with ink.

"It's probably for the best that it was destroyed," he muttered, pinching at a corner and taking it from me. "I have it all memorized, anyway." He added as he threw it into the blazing fire that burned in the fireplace nearby.

We were silent for a moment, giving me a chance to mop up the ink before it dried. The ink seemed to pool on the table in a peculiar shape my eyes failed to make sense of. The black liquid resembled the shape of a bird. *An omen?* I covered it with the rag, disregarding the idiotic thought. *It's just spilled ink.* I reminded myself. Though when I removed the cloth, the faint stain of a bird in flight still lingered.

I stood next to Logan as we stared at the dancing tendrils of flame. Licking at the edges until it ignited. Listening to the crackle and pop of the wood below as the fire grew hotter and brighter. Both of us were silent as the corners curled and the parchment paper blackened.

"Mama!" Felix whined loudly, cutting through the silence like a hot knife in butter. He broke out into loud, unconsolable sobs moments later. It was clear by the glassy sheen of Logan's eyes that he too, composed as he was, longed for Cassidy's return. Their fear and worry tugged at my heartstrings while my guilt gnawed away at my insides. *I should have been there. If I had not swapped my duties, Cassidy would be here. I would rather die than let anything happen to her.*

Plagued by my selfishness, I struggled to look at Logan and Felix. My words clawing my throat as if I was spitting razors instead. "Your Grace... Logan... we have searched every inch of the castle and its grounds. There was no sign of her... no clue to what happened... where she could have gone."

"Cassidy was *taken*, Flynn." Logan hissed, walking across the room to the large, arched window that viewed the courtyard and the vast fields stretching across most of Eyre until the line of evergreen trees blocked the rest of the view. Many years ago, those trees had been the boundary of the battlefield; securing the place where many innocent people fought in the war. A war raged out of love and desire for one woman's heart–*Cassidy's*.

I felt the pit in my stomach open wider as I picked through my memories. Recounting the last moments where Cassidy's mind connected with mine. Seeing for the first time what Cassidy had seen moments before her sudden disconnect: the shadows of the courtyard. The blooming flowers swayed in the breeze. A crow standing on the lawn, statuesque-still.

The small hairs on the back of my neck stood on end and a chill ran down my spine. The bird-like stain and the crow Cassidy saw could not be a coincidence. *There is no such thing as coincidences.* It was only when Cassidy was walking back to the castle did I notice the shadow take the form of a person. Looming over Cassidy from behind, getting larger as it drew closer.

I gulped as bile rose in my throat. "*Shifters?*" I gasped, my attention snapping back to Logan. "I know what happened... but you're not going to like it."

SEVENTEEN

Everything in the world was silent. My eyes studied the figure before me, dug up from its recent grave. Ashen gray skin, paper-thin and fragile. Long white hair that had lost its glossy sheen the moment its owner's life was snubbed.

The Phantom promised this would work. I need it to work. She is the only person aside from Cassidy that I could trust. She must return to me. Her resurrection was not only for my selfish gain, so I did not have to mourn her loss, but it was an experiment. If successful, this plan would help me displace my brother on his throne. A plan hatched out of hatred and defeat would be how I would take back what is mine for good. *What I need was an army. An army of the dead.*

The more I thought about that day I lost it all, the more bitter the taste become in the back of my throat. *"All wrongs can be righted, my son."* my father had once told me. *But I am toiling a dark path, one I fear can never be undone.*

My father would never have approved of what I have done. Logan would be mortified, *and Cassidy will hate me.* Such a disturbing and grotesque act to bring the daughter, whom he hated, back to life. I watched in nervous anticipation as the necromancer got to work. Sharpening his blade against the grindstone before heading my way.

I gulped, catching the glint of the razor-sharp edge in the moonlight. There was not a single cloud in the sky; the air was so cold and crisp it made my breaths linger in the air like fog.

"Close your eyes." The Phantom's voice whispered in my mind, causing my grip to tighten on the bundle I was holding. Feeling it wriggle and squirm against the increased pressure. A small whimper escaped its mouth. It was almost as if it knew crying out loud was hopeless. Accepting its fate. We were too far from any civilization for anyone to hear its wails. No one would come to rescue it. No one other than myself and the necromancer to witness its final breaths.

I kept my eyes open. I was not stupid to place my trust in the necromancer, especially when he was holding a blade. I leaned to my side, reassured by the cool blade of my dagger grazing my thigh and my sword sheath hitting my knee. *I need to keep my wits as sharp as that blade;* I thought as he loomed over me. His ominous presence cast me in shadow. *One flick of his wrist and I could end up like Demi.*

Dark eyes peered up at me, pleading with me to reconsider; to change my mind before it was too late. But one glance over at my sister's corpse. I knew that this was bigger than the baby in my arms. Bigger than my sister–if this plan worked, this small sacrifice would be worth it. *And if it doesn't,* I shook my head, *well... I will find another way.*

The blade sliced through the air in one swift motion. Soft gurgling sounds filled the silence, echoing in my ears and churning my stomach. Blood spurted from the clean cut; sprays of crimson covered me. Splattering on my face and on the necromancer's mask. Years ago, at the Masquerade of Whispers, I selected a mask similar to his. I wanted that power; to be feared like he was. The twisted desire to wield a soul and to play god. *I want to decide who lives and who dies.*

The droplets trickled down the white plastic cheeks as I watched with a mixture of fascination and repulsion. Entranced by the vibrant scarlet smear left behind as his cloaked arm wiped across the mask. I heard the heavy thump and the snapping of twigs as the necromancer dropped the blade to the ground. Placing the ceramic bowl beside my hand that was now warm and wet as the blood pumped from the wound.

My stomach churned. Glancing down for the first time at the bloody mess in my arms. The white blanket that swaddled the child was now stained and sticky to the touch. The distinct metallic scent lingered in my nostrils. *I had to do this.* I told myself over and over, ignoring the blood still pouring from its neck. *I have to get her back.*

"Are you talking about your sister... or the Queen?" The Phantom asked silently, tilting his head as his black soulless eyes bore into mine. It was a rhetorical question. He already knew the answer. The reason I was going to such macabre measures. *Everything I do, I*

am doing for her-Cassidy. The blood from the child slowed, taking with it the once pink glow from the child's cheeks.

I never cared much for children. I never wanted my own. They were nothing but leeches - of my time and my freedom. Yet the moment I learned Cassidy was pregnant with Logan's child, I wished it was mine. Feeling my jealousy unleash within like a feral green-eyed monster. Furious and uncontrollable. It had been the fuel that had driven me to snatch this child sleeping from its crib besides its parents. I imagined it as their child. It was easier that way. Living out my dream to erase every trace of Logan from Cassidy's life once I get her back. *She will always be mine. I do not want her tainted child being a constant reminder of my failure. Nor do I want anything other than her undivided attention.*

"We are done with the child." The Phantom said, drifting over to Demi. I could not see her face in the darkness, only the outline of her body as it lay among the trampled leaves of the woodland floor. She was wearing a floral summer dress; a dress that in life she would never have worn. But it was something from Alyiah's wardrobe or the dress she had died in–bloodied and torn. I smirked. *Demi would have complained either way.*

As the necromancer drew symbols over her exposed skin, the child's body felt like a ton of bricks in my arms. The burden of my choice weighed heavily on my chest. "What should I do with *this?*" I asked, refusing to look down once more.

"Take it deeper into the woods. The wolves will take care of it." His voice hissed in my mind, annoyed that I had interrupted him. I nodded, dragging my eyes away from him as he floated around her body. His footsteps were inhumanly quiet. Not a single leaf on the ground moved, yet his robe rustled as he hovered around Demi's body.

How much farther should I go? I asked myself, forcing each foot in front of the other. The branches full of leaves formed a dense canopy overhead. Blocking out the silver moonlight until I could barely see a few feet in front of me. The woods here were writhing with wildlife, the flapping of bats' wings and the hoots of owls. When the sudden howl of a wolf, sounding too close for comfort, reverberated on the wind. *I think this is far enough.*

Dumping the child at the base of the closest tree, I backed off hurriedly. My steps quickly becoming a sprint the moment I heard more paws approach the bundle of blankets. Their heavy, animalistic pants turned into snarls and howls. That was when I heard it, the sickening snapping of bones and tearing of flesh. Sounds that would forever haunt me until my dying days. *I had to do it.* I told myself. *This is nothing compared to what is coming.*

The piercing scream shattered my thoughts as birds in the trees squawked violently; abandoning their nests without hesitation. *Demi.* My feet pounded against the floor. Faster and faster with each moment. Her scream continued. The last time I had run this fast was with Cassidy by my side as we rushed to rescue Jace from Elder Xion's hateful wrath.

I thought about that night often, her acceptance of my help over Logan's. It had given me hope that her decision had been made. That deep down she wanted to choose me but could not bring herself to admit it. *I could give her the life she had always wanted. I could teach her how to stretch her wings and be free.*

My thoughts snapped back to Alyiah. She was just a means to an end. Pretty, attractive and very *satisfying*, but she would never hold a flame to Cassidy. *But she has to believe that she will, so does her father.*

I reached the small clearing in the woods, seeing her white skeletal hands clutch at the ground, crushing handfuls of dirt into her clenched fists. Witnessing her back arch unnaturally while her legs and toes flexed. That was when she screamed out again. A haunting wail like that of a banshee, coveting my body in goosebumps instantly.

"Does this always happen?" I asked, tentatively approaching, dragging the toes of my tan boots through the mulch.

"Yes... it is the natural reluctance of her body accepting a soul being forced into it." The Phantom responded, stepping aside so that her pale face was now visible. Contorted in sheer agony, her eyes begging for this torture to stop.

I slammed my eyes shut. *I had to do this. I have to do everything I can to take back what is mine.*

EIGHTEEN

Torvus

Holding her head closer to my chest, I prayed that she kept quiet for both of our sakes. Werewolves and Lycans were on the hunt, and I did not have the energy to fend off such beasts. Yet I couldn't blame her. It was not easy news for Cassidy to digest and even harder to accept. Especially to learn from a stranger that her husband and son will die soon. The same stranger who kidnapped her and has been stalking her in his bird-form for the past month.

After a few moments, her sobs quietened. "I don't understand," her voice croaked. She swiped at her tears with the back of her hand, leaving them red and puffy. Her thoughts procured an image of a girl lying face-down in what appeared to be a bathroom stall. Looking down at her as though she were there. But I recognized the gruff voice that panted in the background - Jax.

Is this the girl he is talking about? Her thoughts shrilled. *Who was she? Did she mean something to Torvus? A sister? A girlfriend?*

I shook my head, listening to her other thoughts swirling around her head. Not wanting to believe Jax was capable of such an atrocity. Unwilling to see the fierce determination Jax held to butcher her husband and infant. *Oh, if only you knew.*

"No, someone else... I mean, she was already *technically* dead." I reached out my fingertips and placed them on each temple. "There are others, innocent victims, he has discarded like trash. Collateral damage in the grand scheme of his plan." I paused, watching her chew on her bottom lip. "Although it was not his hands that wielded the blade, his hands will forever remain stained."

The instant my fingertips connected with her skull, I felt her pulse vibrate through them. My fingers seared with fire as I offloaded my memories into her mind.

The gentle breeze carried her floral fragrance in my direction. Tendrils of her white hair whipped at her heart-shaped face. Her piercing eyes shone through the strands with pure determination. The intensity of her glare captivated me; I could not look away. The sun set behind her as we sat on top of the mountainous peak, watching as the full moon began to show itself. I could feel the thrum of her energy, the magic that lay deep within her; ancient magic that did not belong inside her.

For hours, we had been practicing simple spells to help her harness the powers she was cursed with. It was much harder for those not born with the ancient magic to wield it, yet Demi had taken to it like a natural-born mage. I had never, in all my hundreds of years of life, had an apprentice like her.

Over the years, I had grown familiar with her telltale signs of concentration. Noticing how she would flare her nostrils and bite at her bottom lip; her forehead creasing as a scowl knitted her brows together. I had always admired her perseverance, her refusal to become flustered when a spell or enchantment went awry. Instead, her failures fueled her determination to do better, to be better, next time.

The guards were beginning to notice Demi's changing body too, becoming a source of jealousy for me. Anger bristled when I caught them eyeing up her silky legs and her perky, bouncing breasts as she walked. The clothes she wore changed too, more sultry and seductive, encouraging their gaze to her. Deprived of her father's attention, she acquired it from whoever would give it to her. Demi enjoyed the lustful look in their eyes and the indiscreet bulges in their pants. Purposely choosing to saunter past them, flaunting her womanly shape. I heard their minds filling with indecent thoughts. Sickened by the explicit, imaginative acts they wanted the princess to perform. Each one was just as twisted and taboo as my own. It was not proper to imagine the princess on her knees; such impulsive thoughts would warrant a brutal death.

I stalked her like a predator; knowing her every movement. I excused my behavior as care and caution; lies I told myself to lessen the guilt eating away at me. I knew it was wrong of me to fantasize about the princess, yet my feelings for her were more than just lust. I was entranced by her and not merely by her attractive physical qualities. I admired her strength to wield the ancient magic thrust upon her, and found myself drawn to the power she possessed. I adored her kindness when she would let down her guard.

For better or worse, I loved her with every fiber of my being. She was as close to a soulmate as I would ever have.

I never intended to fall in love with her, never expected that she would capture my heart and crawl beneath my skin. For so long, my feelings for her went unnoticed; Demi was too enraptured by the attention of so many than by me. Eventually, she noticed how easily I bent to her whims and would do what she asked without question. The moment she took notice of me, giving me a slither of hope, I broke every rule I had ever made. Notably the number one on my list: *never get involved with an apprentice.*

Before I could stop it, another fond memory occupied my mind. A memory I should never have shared with anyone, for the sake of Demi's reputation and my own.

"Torvus..." Her throaty voice purred in my ear. Her hard nipple beneath her red gown brushed against my arm as her hand reached to my crotch. "I need you." I always felt weak when she said those words; melting beneath her touch.

I was here to chaperone the Masquerade of Whispers. It was my duty to ensure all the guests behaved themselves while within the castle's walls. Yet I found myself watching Demi's every move, as if I was there solely as her protectorate. Jealousy wrapped around my chest like a serpent. Ready to strike at the unfortunate soul who dared to make a move on her. None of them here were good enough for her; no single man alive would ever deserve Demi's love - not even me. However, that did not stop me from secretly wishing she would never find her soulmate; hoping one day she would be mine, and mine alone - in every way.

I should have been in the main hall amid the thrum of the party, not backed into a secluded corridor of the hallway. Breaking up fights and issuing warnings for rowdy behavior. Instead, it was my hard cock threatening to burst beneath her hand. My eyes trained on her cleavage, wanting to release her perky breasts from her tight dress. I gritted my teeth, feeling my resistance falter with every stroke of her thumb over my shielded tip.

Grinding her heat against my leg, she pressed her body against mine, pinning me in place. A devilish smirk curled at her lips as she felt my shaft pushing against the material that held it hostage. She knew exactly what she was doing. Coaxing me to break my vow after our last hook-up. Pushing those buttons that made me lose all self-control. I knew I was on a dangerous and self-destructive path; she would never love me. I wanted her to see me as I saw her. But to her, I was just a means to a very satisfying end.

The yearning in my loins and the lustful thoughts guided my feet as I followed Demi up to her room. The party became nothing more than a distant thrum the higher into the castle we climbed. The moment the door closed behind us, Demi sank to her knees. Her hands were quick to release my hard shaft from its restraints. I shuddered in ecstasy at the sensation of her tongue as it dragged along its length. A moan escaped my lips as she teased the engorged, throbbing head. My hands clutching fistfuls of her hair as her hot mouth enveloped my rigid cock fully.

My heart beat to the rhythm of the base from the party with loud, hard thuds against my ribcage. My breathing came in short, ragged groans as her head bobbed faster and deeper. Teetering the edge of climax as the sound of soft, wet gagging noises filled the room. Demi devoured my manhood with prowess. I was ready to explode in her greedy mouth when she suddenly pulled away. I did not want her to stop. I watched my tormenting angel in annoyance as she wiped away the saliva that dribbled down her chin.

"I want you..." Demi moaned. "I want more of you. I want to make you my chosen mate," she moaned, grinding her bald mound on my fingers.

It was almost surreal: the way my heart leaped at hearing those words I longed to hear, the desperate, possessive way my body reacted to her statement. We had only used our mouths and hands to bring each other pleasure. I never complained, happy to take whatever Demi would offer me. There was no denying, though, that my ultimate fantasy was to sink my shaft deep into her tight, warm slit. Stretching her with my thick, hard cock, making her eyes pop open wide in delight.

"Why?" I asked, removing my fingers from her core. They were coated with her nectar as I dragged them over her lips. Releasing another growl as her lips wrapped around them, sucking her juices off them one by one.

"Because I trust you to take care of me."

I yanked my hand away from Cassidy's temples, my breath catching in my throat. That night had been the first of many nights, all leading to the same mind-blowing ending. Each time finding myself wanting more of her. Before I knew it, I had dug myself a hole too deep to ever get out of.

"You loved her..." Cassidy finally spoke after a few moments of awkward silence; her cheeks flushed deep scarlet and her eyes avoiding mine. She looked every bit as uncomfortable as I felt.

I nodded, moving away from her. My heart was heavy with the knowledge that those memories were all I had left of Demi; the sorrow of losing her all over again hit me like a punch to the gut. "I knew she never truly loved me," I muttered, sitting down on the chair. "I knew she was using me in every way she could to get what she truly wanted... and I let her."

I felt Cassidy's hand on my shoulder. "I'm sorry for your loss, Torvus," she said, her voice soft and sincere. "But Demi's death... that was by her own doing... it was the trolls who killed-"

"I know." I cut her off bitterly. "I was the one who helped her approach the trolls... an action I deeply regret." I took out my penknife and picked up the lump of wood I had been whitling into a sharp point. Trying to keep myself busy, a way to suppress my own anger and self-loathing. *I can never forgive myself for leading her to her demise.*

"But I don't understand... I know what she did was for Jax... but she, um... it wasn't exactly Jax's fault... She was his sister, his twin, he was... *is*... distraught by her death," Cassidy said, trying to select her words carefully.

"No, it wasn't his fault...*the first time.*" My eyes snapped up to hers, feeling the venom seep through my final words. Her brows knitted together, tilting her head to one side, her face displaying the confusion that plagued her thoughts.

Her blank stare told me she knew very little of what Jax had been up to this past couple of years. "Cass... I thought Logan would have told you. I mean, he must have known about it..." I saw a flicker of anger dancing in her eyes like a small flame as she continued to stare at me.

The muscles in her temple throbbed, and she clenched her jaw. She was hurt and furious, but one of her thoughts stuck with me. *I guess we have both been keeping things from one another.*

Finally, Cassidy spoke through gritted teeth. "Torvus, tell me...what has Jax *done*?"

NINETEEN

He should not have brought her back.

Demi's blank gaze stared out of the window. The sun was rising over the mountains in the distance. She sat unmoving, unblinking and looking every bit as *inhuman* as she felt. The amber glow of the morning sunlight accentuated her gaunt face and reflected in dull eyes set in sunken sockets. I missed the fire that burned behind them, the intensity and drive that made them sparkle.

I sighed. *He should never have bought Demi back from the dead.* Gone was the woman I had loved; with smooth, sleek hair and a breath-taking smile. Now, her thin and wispy strands of hair hung limp over her shoulders.

Only a few months had passed since her reanimation, she was not supposed to decline so rapidly. The babe Jax had sacrificed was fit and healthy; a soul set to live for several decades. Yet, here Demi was, zombified and silent, neither living nor dead.

I took a step backwards, nauseousness creeping up on me as the stench of death clung to my nostrils. Her flesh rotten, strips of her once beautiful porcelain skin hung from limp bones. My stomach lurched, bile rising in my throat as a piece of skin slid from her cheekbone and fell to the floor with a sickening thud.

I took another silent step backwards, not wanting her to notice my presence. I could not bring myself to be in the same room as her. The gentle breeze that drifted from the slight crack of the open window carried the aroma of her corpse. My stomach churned as I thought back to the conversation I had overheard last night. The Phantom explained to

Jax there was only one explanation for Demi's deterioration; Demi was refusing to accept the new soul. Jax had thrust his decision unwillingly into her.

"I want to go back," Demi suddenly spoke. Her voice was barely a whisper. "I want to go back to the darkness... to w-w-where I *belong*." Her head whipped around to face me, her glazed eyes filled with sorrow and melancholy.

Until this point, I was uncertain how much of her own soul she had retained and if her decaying body still possessed emotions as she would have in life. So far, her new life has consisted of following Jax's every command. A lab rat in Jax's experiment, forced to do his bidding and to test the boundaries of her body's capabilities. He wanted to learn all he could from her, so that Jax could prepare to make more just like her.

Time after time, Jax would test her strength, pushing his undead soldier to the limit. He became desensitized to the stench of decomposition; unaffected when more chunks of her flesh worked its way loose from her bones.

I had stood by as Jax had ordered Demi to slaughter men in busy taverns because they disagreed with him or worse; they still honored an allegiance with King Logan. I had not intervened when she stole sleeping babies from their cribs with no hesitation or emotion. It was why I believed she was incapable of feeling such things.

The idea of bringing her back from the afterlife had repulsed me. From the very first moment the thought entered his mind, I knew I should have stopped him. *I should have known nothing good ever came from defying nature.*

Instead, I looked on with a selfish hope that she would come back to me. Days before her death, she had *chosen* me to be her mate. She *wanted* me, and in her own way, *loved* me. It was hard to accept that all she and the future I so desired was gone forever.

"Come... c-come closer," Demi hissed; her skeletal fingers beckoning me to her. "*Please.*"

My heart throbbed in my ears and goosebumps pricked my skin as I closed the gap between us. My steps were heavy and cumbersome, as if wearing lead boots. The inflection of her dialect reminded me of the many times she had coerced me into helping her before the War. I knew she was plotting to destroy Logan and Cassidy, yet I clutched to the naïve hope that it was for *our* future. Not because she still loved and *wanted* her twin.

"You are not foolish..." She muttered, her eyes bore into mine. For the first time since her reanimation, I could see something flicker in her glazed eyes, revealing that she could feel *everything*. "But I need you to... to do something... for me... *one last time.*"

Her hand grabbed mine with a fierce and unnaturally strong grip. Her forehead pressed against mine. I had not noticed the dagger in her hand until it was suddenly thrust into my own.

"I c-can't..." I shook my head as tears streamed down my face.

"If you truly loved me, you would let me go..."

I thrust the blade into her chest, letting my tears spill as it sank deeper. Feeling as it pierced her heart, animated only by dark spells and blood magic. I twisted the blade, imagining it tearing through Jax's heart. *I want him to hurt as I do.*

I felt her arm drop from mine and her body slump forward. My hand trembled as I let go of the handle, unable to believe what I had just done. I did not regret it; but I was feeling the loss and pain of losing Demi all over again because of *Jax*. It was his fault. *He* is the reason I lost her a second time.

My legs trembled as I turned away from her. My heart felt just as heavy as my feet as I forced one in front of the other as I left her behind. Glancing at her one last time over my shoulder, the sight of her lifeless body brought white-hot tears to my eyes. I did not want to leave her like that, she deserved to be laid to rest with dignity, yet I could not stay. I tried to appease the guilt that plagued me as I stepped out into the street; telling myself over and over that it had been her choice – her last wish. I held onto the notion that I had prevented her prolonged suffering; that I had helped her to find peace. The cold squeezed the air from my lungs, each step becoming heavier, pausing for a moment to gather up the last of my strength. My gaze casting upwards as I drew in a deep breath. The sky was now streaked with scarlet, vibrant and angry. It was almost poetic; *the sky was bleeding because Demi's body could not.*

I cast one last glance over my shoulder at her slumped silhouette in the window. *I need to be as far away as possible. Jax will notice the macabre scene soon enough, and he will know I am to blame.*

I thought of the furthest and most unexpected place to be. Somewhere no one would dare venture. I clicked my fingers. Disappearing from the streets of Verancas into the silence and darkness.

Moments later, I was on the very mountain that had obscured the sunrise from Demi's view. I stood on the peak of Mount Hejha, the sun blindingly bright as tears rolled down my cheeks. I had come here to our training spot with a fierce determination to fulfill Demi's final wish - to end this war once and for all. I knew I could not do it alone, after what I had done I could not get close enough to Jax by myself. *I will need help.*

An idea sprung into my mind, a vision of an unlikely ally of my own - the one person who could get close enough to Jax without raising any suspicion - *Cassidy*.

TWENTY

Cassidy

I stifled a gasp, biting my lip until the metallic taste of blood filled my mouth as I watched Torvus' memories of Demi as a grotesque, re-animated corpse instead of how I saw her last, filled with fire and pride. I looked on in horror as I saw her bedraggled body limp through the streets. Her limp, fleshless arms smuggling screaming babies inside their swaddles of blankets; taking them to *him*. Hearing their wails echo as she took them to the woods; their cries reverberating even louder the deeper into the thick brush of trees she wandered.

Torvus never could bring himself to watch what happened next; turning his back on it all the moment Demi disappeared from his sight. But it was clear - those babies were never returning to their families.

Torvus trudged through the streets. Averting his gaze from the windows of the houses Demi had visited. He knew those parents would be forever tormented by questions. Wracked with guilt at their failure to protect their most vulnerable family member. Always plagued with uncertainty - never knowing why. Trying to muddle through the rest of their lives, unaware their child had been used in a sacrificial ritual to raise an undead army.

"The truth would only have hurt them more," Torvus said, his glassy eyes unable to meet mine. "I could do nothing to stop her..." He lifted his sleeve, revealing a long, jagged silver scar spanning from his shoulder to his wrist. "She was following *commands*. Instructed to destroy anyone that tried to stop her from fulfilling his demands."

My cheeks were wet. Tears had rolled down my cheeks unwittingly as I watched the scenes play out. My stomach twisted into knots, and the repulsive tang of bile filled my throat.

Betrayal weighed heavy on my chest. *Why had Logan kept this from me?*

"I can only assume his intention was to protect you," Torvus murmured, handing me a box of tissues from the table. "Jax has gotten himself mixed up with some dangerous people, Cass. Pirates, rogue traders, fugitives and now the necromancer..."

A veil of silence cloaked us making the air feel thick and heavy. The only sound that could be heard was the faint whistle of the wind outside. Both of us sat uncomfortably, staring at the floor between us.

"The people Jax thinks are *supporting* him will have their own agendas. All wanting to gain something from his defeat over King Logan." Torvus finally spoke, feeling his gaze pointed in my direction watching as I flinched at the idea. I could not bring myself to look his way, still shocked and disgusted that Logan would be part of such heinous atrocities.

Torvus leaned forward in his seat, his hands clasped together. "The necromancer is not helping Jax build an army of undead soldiers out of the kindness of his heart, that's for sure."

I nodded slowly. I had only ever heard about the myth of the Phantom; only every thought of him as the villain depicted in childrens' cautionary tales; an evil, child-snatcher who would steal naughty children refusing to sleep at bedtime. My stomach lurched, feeling stupid and naïve. *How many more storybook creatures were real?*

Torvus' eyebrows raised in surprise. A small, amused smirk played on his lips. "You have never been beyond Estoria, have you?"

I felt my humiliation graduate into anger. "I have actually," I snapped, folding my arms across my chest. Trying to suppress the memories I had of the places I had traveled with Jax, our intimate moments, knowing Torvus could read my thoughts. Yet, that morning in Trikara, watching the sunrise over the hills with Jax's head buried between my thighs would not go away.

Torvus coughed loudly. "I think you'll find Jax is a little *different* these days." His tone was clipped.

He moved over to a large closet set along the furthest wall from where I was sitting. For several long minutes, he kept his back to me; preventing me from seeing what he was doing, only hearing the clinking of glass bottles as he searched for something.

"So tell me, Torvus, what other creatures exist? Werewolves? Centaurs? Banshees? Dragons and Flufflegumps?" Though my question was intended as a joke, judging from the way Torvus' body froze, I knew the humorous jest had been lost on him.

"Never ask a question you fear the answer to." He sighed. "Werewolves, yes. Centaurs, yes. Banshees, *definitely*. But sadly, the Flufflegumps were eaten by the last of the dragons, who are now themselves extinct. *Thanks* to the Silverthorne family." I nodded, though I did not understand. *How did I not know any of this?*

"The truth, Cassidy, is that you only know what the Elders *want* you to know. It's why they restrict travel so much beyond Eyre. Especially Estorians... you live too much of a sheltered life to live among the rest of the world they abandoned."

Torvus spun on his heel to face me, holding three small glass vials. Each one filled with a clear liquid with a syrupy viscosity. I watched the silky, shimmering contents inside the bottle swirling in anticlockwise circles.

"What are those?" I asked, my eyes transfixed on the bottles as he made his way back towards me.

"These are your failsafe. Your *last resort*." His voice was quiet, but his face belied his seriousness. "Cassidy, you must help me stop, Logan. *This* is the quickest and most painless death known to man..." he paused, holding out a bottle to me. "*Subita morte,* its literal translation is sudden death. Odorless and colorless, the unfortunate drinker cannot detect what is to come."

The vial in my hand felt warm to the touch, its heat rapidly increasing with every second it lay in my palm. "Take it back," I hissed, not wanting to move. "Please." I added quickly, noticing his hesitancy. He nodded, holding it by the black wax-covered stopper. His fingers delicately laid them inside a small velvet-lined wooden box.

Silence enveloped us once more while his words dawned on me. "I can't... you can't expect me to..." I stuttered, refusing to take the wooden box Torvus was offering to me.

"You are the only person who can get that close to him." Torvus sighed, still offering the wooden box in his outstretched hand. "If you give that to Jax, everything stops. Your son, your husband... their fate is not yet set in stone *if* we can stop Jax. We will need to do it soon. Before he makes a deal with the witches of Halen. I fear, once he has their protection, it will be too late."

Blood. Lots of it. Sprays of crimson across the walls above two lifeless corpses: One dismembered beyond recognition, the other heartbreakingly devoid of its heart. The world shifted on its axis, knocking me to the floor. My knees sodden and my hands covered in the blood of the

two people who meant everything to me. Without them, I had nothing. Without them,
the world was dull and monotonous, cold and cruel.

I could not bring myself to look before; to find my husband's severed head. The
compulsion to see his face once more overpowered every other thought. That was when
I found it, his hair clutched in the monster's fist, who delivered such a barbaric act in
the name of 'love'. The monster who held the heart of my only child in its other hand.

Fire spread through me; scorching through my chest and incinerating my lungs.
It was only when Torvus' hands grabbed me, covering my mouth, did I realize I had
been screaming. "I'm going to let go of you now, but you *must* stop screaming before
you get us both killed."

I nodded, feeling his grip loosen. "I'm sorry that you had to see that, but *that* is
what awaits you, should you refuse to help me."

Torvus planted an image in my mind. The sight of me pouring the contents of
one vial into Logan's glass of water while his back was turned. Adding another into
my son's bottle of milk before I tucked him into bed. Perching on the edge of our
own bed, watching and waiting for them both to take a sip. Logan's body slumped
forward, his head hitting the pillow hard. Felix's eyes fluttering open, now suddenly
dull and unblinking. Unable to feel the rise and fall of his chest against me as he
drank.

No, I can't do that. Logan's security detail will do their jobs.

Torvus cleared his throat, stirring me from my thoughts and directing my attention back to him. "Cass, if *I* managed to breach the security detail... it would all be
too easy for the Phantom..."

"But you, you are, were, a *crow*... Logan wouldn't be expecting *shifters*."

"As King, Logan should be anticipating *everything*. He should be preparing for
even the unlikeliest of foes." He paused, the weight of his words sinking in. "*Shifters*
can only be one animal, the one they are born with. I can only become a crow."
Before my eyes, he plucked a glossy black feather from thin air. "But the myth that
surrounds The Phantom is that he can be *anything* he wants..."

I looked around to the door, angsty and impatient, stomping towards it. "I must
warn him..."

I threw open the door, not sure what I was expecting to see. It certainly was not
mountainous terrains, with large evergreen trees. Everything in sight was covered with a
thick dusting of snow. The air was thick with amber fog as it dimmed the light from the

rising sun to my left. The scene before me stopped me in my tracks. *Where the fuck are we?*

"Mount Hejha," Torvus said suddenly behind me.

"Mount Hejha?" I asked skeptically, my eyes dancing across the landscape, feeling the urge to step on the crisp, untouched snow beyond the threshold. I took a step, and then another, my breath taken away by the view. Torvus' hands tried to grasp my wrist, to stop me, but I shook them off.

"How far up are we?" I asked, briefly glancing over my shoulder at him. Torvus looked worried, as his head swept from side to side as he made his way over to me.

"It is not safe out here. The terrain is unstable and rocky beneath the snow." He said, keeping pace as I moved closer to the edge, "Plus, there are creatures that live here-" His words trailed off as I pushed forward. My eagerness to see more taking over.

I lost my footing, not noticing a loose stone hidden by the blanket of white. My foot snagged it and I stumbled. Instinctively, I screamed as I fell forwards.

It echoed for miles, reverberating through the dense fog and ringing in my ears. The air was thin this high up, my head spinning at the lack of oxygen. My lungs stinging as I struggled to breath, unable to expand fully as I gulped frantically. The icy bite of the snow chilled me to the bone as I lay there too stunned to speak. My head was inches from the edge of the cliff. I had come so close to plummeting to my death. *Jax would, at least, no longer have a reason to continue sacrificing innocent children.*

Torvus stood beside me, offering his hand out to help. His brow knitted together as a frown deepened on his face. With shaky hands, I took it. Feeling goosebumps prick my skin as I gazed at the object I had tripped over. It was not a rock after all - it was a human skull.

"We are higher up than Death's Ridge," Torvus said, his hand clinging to mine. "Any who wander beyond that point there," he pointed to a small ledge a little lower on the mountain, "are guaranteed to perish. Being almost six-thousand feet above sea level, it is usually the cold that attacks the body first, then issues arise from the lack of oxygen in the atmosphere. That is... if the werewolves who have lost all of their humanity, who stalk this terrain, haven't gotten to them first."

I looked out across the horizon. Verancas and the other kingdoms looked like nothing but settlements for ants. Shapeless blobs of the buildings below, the sea stretching end-lessly beyond them. The dense fog seemed to get thicker, making it difficult to pick out the borders of each kingdom. It seemed surreal to be almost on top of the world, looking down upon them like a god.

"Cass, we better get back inside." Torvus said, his head scanning the wasteland behind us. He yanked on my wrist, pulling me back towards the hut. Reluctantly, I followed, feeling a fire spread through my body with each breath I took. My head was dizzy and unable to focus on a singular thought.

A howl ripped through the air as a large black shadow emerged from behind the thick trunk of an evergreen tree. Through the fog, all I could notice was its sheer size, shaggy fur and long claws as it stalked closer on two legs. I stared at the creature. "Torvus, is that a-"

"Yes" He hurriedly dragged me the last few steps, pushing me through the open door and slamming it shut. Another howl, louder, *closer*. "We must leave."

I perched against the back of the couch as he flitted from one side of the room to the other. Frantically gathering items and throwing them into a brown leather satchel. His eyes resting on the wooden box that had been left on the side table. "Take them, Cass..." he murmured.

I reached forward, my fingertips brushing the cool polished box. I tried not to think about how dangerous the contents were inside. I was about to protest when the door flung off its hinges behind me.

It collided into the stone wall with such force the wooden door fractured and splintered. I gasped, catching sight of the crimson eyes of the beast. Hearing the ghastly snap of jaws of sharp teeth as it snarled at us. Then came a thunderous growl that resonated from its chest.

I knew I should run, but was frozen in fear as my scream caught in my throat. *This was not how I imagined I would die.* I thought, my hands losing its grip on the box of vials. My eyes strayed from the beast momentarily, looking for Torvus. But he was gone, a crow in the place he once stood. His beady black eyes staring from me to the satchel.

I lunged for it just as the creature pounced. Narrowly missing his claws as they swiped in my direction. Slicing through the thin material of my clothes and drawing blood. The werewolf seemed to enjoy tormenting us. Licking its lips at the sight of crimson spreading across my back.

It turned on its heel away from us, raking its claws along the shelves. One by one, it knocked over the glass jars, sneering as they shattered on the floor. When it spun around to face us once more, its teeth were bared, ready for the kill-strike.

Torvus, in his crow form, took flight, swooping through the air. Its talons poised, embedding into its eyes seconds later.

The beast yelped in agony, its claws flailing in the air, trying to catch the bird. But Torvus was fast, pulling away from the beast with both eyeballs tightly clutched in each talon. The creature folded in on itself, falling through the wooden table with an almighty crash. Its vibrations shook the earth, creating an even louder rumble beyond the walls of Torvus' hut.

"We need to go. Now."

In a cloud of swirling purple smoke, I watched as the hut spun before my eyes. The shattered glass beneath the werewolf's limp body disappeared from view; swallowed by a black abyss that threatened my vision. I blinked, trying to clear it, but it was in vain; all I could see was darkness. Nothing but a never ending void of pitch black. *Is this how my life, and the war, ends?*

TWENTY ONE

Logan

I will not stop, not until I find Cassidy. I stared into the hazel eyes of my advisor, Esan, his exasperated expression I knew only too well. *I must look like shit.*

My body was worn out, beyond the point of exhaustion, in my efforts to find her. Scouring every part of Estoria on foot along with the search parties. My chest ached without her close, our bond tugging my heart in all directions as it tried to seek her out. My soul searched for its mate.

"Sire, it has been seven hours. You must rest..." Esan paused, noticing the glare I was giving him. He quickly changed tack. "I mean, you will be of no use to the Queen if you're dead after running yourself ragged in your search for her."

I nodded. He was right. *He always is.* "There is one place I want to look again," I sighed. "If she is not there, I will yield to your command."

"Where the two of you first met?" He asked, waiting for my response. Esan knew very little about the place Cassidy and I had first met. The lake. *Our sacred place.* The one place in Estoria I did not need to rebuild after the war. "Haven't you been there several times already? This secret location no-one, not even I, can search with you?"

I nodded once more, slower this time. I had been sure I would have found her there. In the past, she gravitated back to the serenity of the lake. I was dumbfounded when I arrived to find it empty. Every visit since, a desperate plea in case she had eventually returned. Yet it tore another chunk from my heart when I came back to the castle without her.

"I do not feel comfortable letting you go on your own, Your Highness," Esan started. "Would you reconsider allowing myself to come with you?" He knew the answer would be a resounding no, as it had been the last time and the time before that.

I shook my head. Hanging back as the search party we were with began leaving the borough of Fic. My reluctance to allow Esan to escort me to the lake also stemmed from pride. For the short amount of time I was there, I could let the facade on my face slip; I could let my tears fall freely. While I was alone at the lake, I no longer had to be the strong, resilient King. I could just be Logan; a boy who loved and missed a girl.

My heart thrummed, and my palms were slick as I entered the thrush of trees. Winding and weaving my way through them, I noticed that the ground was slightly worn. Our footsteps had scarred the earth; taking the same route for all these years had carved a path in the mud and moss.

She has to be here, I told myself, marching forward. The crunch of dried leaves underfoot drowned out the background melody of birdsong.

"*Cassidy... Cass... if you can hear me; please come home.*" Silence. Deafening and ominous.

Ahead, the outline of the lake was just visible. The tree trunks were more sporadic here, stretching their canopy of leaves overhead. The last of the sunlight flooding through the gaps, illuminating the way forward. Not that I needed guidance; I could navigate these woods with my eyes closed for the amount of times we come here.

I took a deep breath, feeling my lungs expand until they could no more, before stepping out into the clearing. Allowing them to deflate as my eyes raked the lake's edge; scanning the long grassy banks and the wild blooms.

Cassidy was not here.

Instinctively, my feet continued to carry my deflated self to the lake's edge. I reached the same part we always stood. A small piece of land jutted into the lake more than the rest of the bank. Unable to walk any further, unable to hold myself upright, I dropped to my knees like a ton of stone.

Without Cassidy, I could not appreciate the beauty of my surroundings. It was the awe in her eyes as the chorus of wildlife greeted us that truly made this place come alive. This was *her* lake, her little sanctuary that she kindly shared with me. I felt lost here without her; this place was empty in her absence.

Peering down into the calm surface of the lake, my face stared back at me; as clear and crisp as a mirror. Dark shadows circled my bloodshot and weary eyes. My hair was damp with sweat. The torture of not knowing what happened to Cassidy was obvious in my reflection. *No wonder why Esan looked concerned; I look half-dead.*

My mind went back to one of the first reports sent to me that detailed Jax's whereabouts and activities. The contents of the letter made me nauseous. I almost ripped it up in disbelief. Yet I could not stop myself from reading more. The words 'sacrifice', and 'necromancer' leaped off the page. Guilt struck like a chord in my chest. *I had not told her. because Jax still had a connection to her.*

The wind gently whistled through the trees, harmonizing with the chorus of cicadas. The colors of fall were more prominent here than anywhere else in Estoria. Leaves of yellows, coppers, and crimson clutched to branches until it was their time to fall. The long grass littered with dried brown leaves at the base of their trunks. There was an icy-bite to the air as darkness crept across the sky. *Winter will be here soon, stripping away life from nature, leaving only bare bones.*

A shiver ran down my spine. The vast emptiness wrapped around me like a shroud. There was no escaping the void Cassidy left. Even Felix could feel her absence, though too young to understand. He would wake howling for his mama; yearning for her gentle touch and longing to hear the softness in her voice as she soothed him back to sleep. Felix used to settle immediately in my arms, calmed by my dulcet tones and firm grip. But since Cassidy's disappearance, I could not console him.

Back in the castle under Flynn's capable watch, I had left Felix sleeping. I was determined to join every search party until she was found. *I should really get back to him.* Yet my body refused to move, paralyzed, as I continued staring at my reflection. Those last moments with Cassidy replaying in my mind.

There had been no reason for her to leave of her own accord. Everything had been perfect - as it always was between us. Cassidy had fallen asleep in my arms with her lips curled in a satisfied grin - no different from every other night. I wracked my brain trying to recall our conversation as doubt and regret seeped into my thoughts. *Did I tell her I love her?*

I leaned forward, my fingers digging deep into the soil as I let go of the tears I had been holding back. Alone. Lost. *Empty.*

It was difficult to contain these emotions with all eyes upon me. Burdened with the weight of the Kingdom on my shoulders while my heavy heart filled with dread. With each hour that passed, the longer Cassidy was missing, the more people were watching me, waiting for me to crumple. I continued to bark orders, suppressing my fear and replacing it with authority. I could not show them my weakness, but here, without their eagle-eyes stalking me, I let it all out.

Free from their judgement, and prying eyes, but their unspoken questions lingered in the air. *Did Cassidy run away to be with Jax? Had she changed her mind?*

I refused to accept this. I tried, at the very least to convince myself she had not gone to him willingly. Regret sank like a stone in the pit of my stomach as I chided myself for not telling her of the evil he has done. *Would she have believed me?*

I shook my head. Cassidy always saw the good in everyone, no matter what. *"Cassidy, where are you?"* I tried to reach out to her telepathically once more. Anxiety gnawed at my insides as the sinking feeling of failure settled into my bones. The blockade that surrounded her thoughts still held strong.

A crow's caw startled me. My eyes snapped open, gazing across to the other side of the lake. I studied the swift movements of the bird mid-flight. Picking out the dark blur as it soared the sky until it became nothing more than a black dot in the sky. Within seconds, it had completely vanished.

It was only when my eyes dropped back to the lake that they caught a figure standing on the opposite side. *My eyes are playing tricks on me*, I thought as I rubbed them, swatting at the tears that clung to my lashes. *They are making me see what I want to see.*

It was almost identical to the first time I saw her. Standing at the lake's edge, the hem of her lace dress fluttering in the wind. Her dark curls dancing on the breeze behind her. Yet, this time my mind had dressed her in what I had last seen her in; a dusky pink nightdress of the finest silk. *Why would I envision her wearing her patented black 'Mary Jane' shoes with her nightgown?*

I blinked again, forcing myself to take a proper look at the figure. *Could it really be her?*

A shockwave quaked through me to the core; her thoughts and feelings flooded through me: Love, fear, *pain.* Invisible cords bound us together once more, stitching up the gaping hole in my heart. *My soulmate.*

"Logan!" How I had longed to hear her voice calling my name like a sweet melody. I watched in shock for a few moments as the figure moved, running in my direction. By the time I scrambled to my feet, she was already halfway.

"Cass!" I shouted. My voice echoed loudly, disturbing the birds' peaceful tunes in the nearby trees. Excitement, anticipation and adrenaline coursed through my body. My heart pounded hard against my ribcage. *She is safe! She is here!*

Dragging my cumbersome feet, I charged towards her, the two of us now only feet from each other. Suddenly Cassidy pounced; her arms and legs cocooned me. Gripping me with every ounce of strength she had while she buried her head into the crook of my neck. Her sudden propulsion caused us both to tumble onto the long grass. The sudden scent of the wild blooms and her familiar fragrance filled my nostrils.

I never wanted to let go. *Am I dreaming?* Yet when Cassidy's lips found mine, I knew this was not a dream.

"Logan..."

I cut her off with another kiss, wanting nothing more than to savor this moment. Rolling on top of her so that I could look at her properly. My eyes scanned every part of her face; losing myself in those green eyes of hers.

"Cass..." I whispered, brushing her hair out of her eyes, still in disbelief that she was here. "I thought I had... that you were-" I gasped as I kissed her neck, trailing up to her plump lips. "I... I..."

She silenced me with a kiss, deepening it with her tongue in its frantic search for mine. Arching her back, nails digging deep into my shoulders, she pressed herself against me. My shaft was awake and ready for her.

I groaned loudly, wanting her, *needing* her. Shifting my weight onto my metal limb so that the other could slip beneath the hem of her silk dress. Cassidy gasped out loud as my fingers traced along her inner thighs. They found her lace underwear, discovering its dampness beneath my fingertips.

Without hesitation, I ripped them away from her body, smirking at the sound of the fabric tearing. I wanted to show her how much I loved her; to make her feel special and *wanted* in every way. Enjoying the feel of her hands threading through my hair as my mouth sealed around her clit. A smile played on my face as she squirmed against my tongue as it lapped at her nectar.

Within moments, she was on the cusp of an orgasm. Her legs squeezed against my shoulders as her orgasm ripped through her body. I did not still my tongue, instead my fingers gripped tightly to the soft flesh of her thighs, holding them open.

"*Logan...*" she purred. I loved the way my name rolled off her tongue as her orgasm left her breathless. It spurred me on. I drew up to kiss her, the longing to sink my solid shaft deep into her, for us to cum in unison.

The moment her warmth enveloped me, our minds and bodies connected. *We are one.* Our connection was strong once more. Sparks of electricity surged through my lips and danced over my skin beneath her touch.

I could not think of anything but her. In this moment we were acting purely on impulse, allowing our natural instincts to take over. Our bodies moved in perfect synchrony.

Cassidy is mine, and I am hers. This is how it will always be.

TWENTY TWO

Fourteen Months Ago
Alyiah

Children were disappearing, faster now than before, like a crescendo of his madness. Under the blanket of darkness, more of them were being snatched from their beds while their unsuspecting parents slept. *We will have to move again.*

I had been dragged from one kingdom to another in an attempt to avoid too much suspicion. The mystery of the abducted children and the loose lips of locals meant fear was rampant. New locks added to doors and windows barricaded with wrought-iron railings did little to deter the undead soldiers. Rumors danced on the breeze and hung heavy in the taverns. Words no one thought they would ever speak in their lifetimes - *The Phantom is back.*

There was nothing anyone could do to stop Jax's skeletal cronies. Time after time, parents tried and failed. If the undead soldiers come in the night for their child, they would take them. Whether they were stolen from their crib or pried from the arms of the slaughtered parents. *The Phantom always gets what he wants.*

I struggled to imagine Jax giving such commands. The charming, carefree, and easy-going guy I had fallen in love with. Sweet, if not a little sarcastic. *It has to be the Phantom,* I told myself firmly. *It has to be my father.* There was a reason my father, the necromancer, was so feared - why he had earned the coined name 'the Phantom.' And it was not only for his ability to resurrect the dead.

I watched in horror as he reappeared before me; his limbs and face manifesting from the thick black smoke that had seeped through a crack in the door. *Speak of the Devil and he shall appear.* As my father materialized before me, I noticed the red splatter on his white, expressionless mask. A strong, metallic stench accompanied him as he stepped forward.

My stomach churned, and a shiver rippled down my spine. Not once had I ever seen his true face; nobody alive had. *Why would my mom consummate with someone as evil as him?*

I shuddered, knowing that the act would not have been voluntary. The thought of this barbaric, inhuman entity impregnating my mother. *I am a monster of his creation.*

I felt his eyes pin me to the spot, felt the thrum of his anger. For a moment, I had forgotten he could read my thoughts. He reached out to me, revealing his blood-stained gloves. *"Blood calls to you, as it does to me."*

I shook my head. A lump formed in the back of my throat and my stomach twisted into knots; telling myself to look away, to not play into the hands of my manipulative father. Yet, I could not deny the lure that the blood of the innocent children had on me as it pooled on the flagstone floors.

"One day, you will cave, my darling daughter. Together, we will be unstoppable."

His body rattled as a low cackle resonated from him, the necklace around his neck jingling together. It was only then that I paid any attention to it, made of teeth, *human* teeth, hundreds of them in various states of decay.

I gulped loudly as he bridged the gap between us, his gloved hand brushing against my cheek. He smeared the still warm blood on my skin in a symbol.

"Such a sweet little bird. You're still growing into your wings." His raspy voice echoed in my skull. *"But you will need to make a decision. Embrace the powers you have inherited; or keep them locked away and remain helpless. Control your destiny, or let others do it for you."*

His hand reached up to his necklace, a trophy taken from every person who had tried and failed to thwart him. *"It would be a pity to add my daughter to this."*

In the blink of an eye, he was gone; disappearing into a puff of smoke. I stepped back, refusing to turn my back on where he had been standing. Unsure if he was really gone, or up to another one of his tricks. *I have to get away from him, from here. Jax has to see sense!*

I could *not* become a monster like him.

Something, or rather *someone,* stopped me from taking another step back. I felt the large figure crash into my spine, a pair of strong and powerful arms wrapped firmly around my torso.

"Alyiah..." A deep gruff voice whispered, their breath hot against my neck. "It is almost time."

"Almost time for what?" I replied, feeling his beard graze against my collarbone as his lips worked their way up to my jaw. "*Jax...*" I purred, my insides squirming at his touch. Each kiss stoked the fire that had ignited within me. His hands slipped around my waist, turning me to face him.

I still had not gotten used to his new look: rough and rugged. His sand-blond hair down to his shoulders, complete with matching beard. Dark ink snaked its way beneath the collar of the t-shirt he wore, bleeding through the pale fabric. His muscles were more prominent and defined; his pale skin was now tanned. All those hours working with the pirates, looting and building ships, had changed him. *Exile had changed him.*

"It is almost time to get my revenge."

Jax's powerful arms drew me in closer, crushing me against his chest. The thrum of his heartbeat vibrated against his ribcage and cast ripples through my own body. My heart fluttered as his mouth inched closer to mine.

I stood on tiptoes to reach them, allowing his hands to slide down my body. Stopping to cup my ass cheeks, using them as leverage to thrust his hips against mine. The solid mass of his shaft pressed against my groin, feeling myself yearn for him. Despite my disgust at recent events, there was no denying my desire for him, my *need* to be with him. *My one real love. My chosen mate.*

"Say it..." he murmured, his nose nudging my cheek.

"I want you... *my King,*" I moaned, his smile widening as his fingers toyed with my damp panties. "Take me now... and make me your *Queen.*"

Something flickered across his eyes, something dark and dangerous. His fingers invading me hard and fast as his thumb worked in circular motions against my clit. Anger seemed to animate him; power was his kink.

I may not have liked *how* he planned to take it back, but I could not wait to reap the rewards. My selfish desire to sit at his side as the Queen. To proudly exclaim that Jax, the most feared and powerful King, was mine. A thought sent ripples along my spine and made the hairs on the back of my neck rise. *But I need Cassidy to die.*

"Is that what you want?" Jax asked. "To fuck the most powerful and *dangerous* King Xeyiera has ever seen?"

"Yes..." I whispered, grinding my hips against his fingers, feeling my orgasm build. "More than anything."

His ego appeased, he thrust another finger inside, his movements rough and violent. "Good girl..." he murmured as my body opened wider for him; encouraging them to go deeper and harder.

Jax's teeth grazed against my earlobe, his hands stilled as I was on the brink of my climax. "But... there is a question of your loyalty." He hissed, slamming his fingers deep into my heat. Hard and brutal. Almost too rough to be enjoyable, *almost*.

A chunk of my hair, now wrapped in his other fist, pulled so hard I thought my neck may snap. "Do I need to clip your wings, little bird? So that you cannot betray me."

I tried to shake my head, but his grip tightened on my hair. "Good, because I *need* you... I need you to keep your father happy... and my *cock*." A deep, throaty groan escaped him as I came. Coating his fingers in my juices that I could not hold back any longer.

"I brought you a gift," he muttered, sinking his teeth into my neck, drawing blood. Licking his lips before shoving his tongue into my mouth. The taste of iron flooded my mouth, along with another distinctive taste that came from Jax's tongue. I could recognize that taste anywhere; *Eleanor*.

"Ah yes... I forgot to mention I already paid her a visit." Jax grinned, licking his lips. "She was delicious." I thrashed against his fingers, my body wracked with jealousy. Eleanor was *my* girlfriend, *our* plaything. There were never any discussions about him spending time with Eleanor *without* me. I went to protest, but Jax yanked on my hair even harder.

I squealed. His fingers ravaged my pussy with a violence that seemed to turn me on more with each second. The hold over my darkness was slipping; the need for more rushing through my veins as I rode his brutish fingers.

"She is here, waiting for you..." he whispered. "But I need to know that you are *mine*." He slid his fingers out as I reached the precipice of another orgasm. "That you will do *whatever* it takes to show me your complete loyalty."

"Anything," I gasped, my slit throbbing in anticipation. I needed my sweet release. I wanted her, but *needed* him. "Jax, you know I will do *anything* for you."

A pair of delicate hands caressed me, starting with my nipples. Pinching and pulling on my hardened peaks until I gasped out loud. I span around to face her, my eyes raking over her deliciously naked body.

Her hips sashayed from side to side, diverting my gaze to the leather strap around her waist. Her smile revealed that her favorite toy was already lodged deep in her pussy. I groaned as she teased the transparent plastic shaft against my clit. Without hesitation, she tugged on my hand, pulling me away from Jax towards the couch. I had a decision to make; *Jax or her?*

My eyes darted between them, lingering on Jax. My hair was still balled in his hands. Without a word, he released me, grabbing his cock in his fist instead. "This is not a test," he groaned, nodding his head slightly. "I want to see her fuck you... to warm up that cunt for me."

His hands pushed me away. I would have fallen had Eleanor's arms not reached out to catch me. There was a look in her eyes, *hatred*. It only lasted a second, but it was long enough for me to notice. Though Jax, his eyes narrowed as his hand stroked his cock, did not.

"Queen Alyiah... it has an ice ring to it." Eleanor said, bitterness tinged her voice. "Shame that there is already a Queen on the throne."

Her lips crushed mine before I could respond. The phallic toy spread my lips apart as she thrust her hips up against my core. Jax's eyes were trained on us, his jaw clenched as he watched me instinctually slam myself down onto it hard. I knew the harder I rode it, the deeper it pushed inside Eleanor's pussy, the more she would buck beneath me. A never-ending circle of hard, fast thrusts that increased the pleasure for both of us.

My moans grew louder, my eyes closing as orgasm after orgasm crashed through me. I was unaware Jax was behind me until I felt his hand push my body forward. Crushing my breasts against Eleanors, unable to move or squirm as he spread my ass cheeks wide. His engorged cock teased my tight asshole.

"Do you remember when Cassidy joined in?" Jax moaned, pushing his rigid shaft inside me inch by inch. I squealed like a pig when I felt his hips jut into my soft, fleshy buttocks. Smacking into me hard and fast as Eleanor bucked beneath me. Both of them claimed me, wanting to be the first to make me scream one of their names.

This must be the test. I thought, as I rode the waves of pleasure. Biting down on my bottom lip hard, too scared that my sex-hazed brain would say the wrong name; make the wrong choice. At that moment, I knew how difficult such a decision was; why Cassidy had refused to make hers.

I felt a prickle of jealousy that spurned into hatred. *Why must he always mention that fucking bitch.* I opened my mouth to speak, but his other hand wrapped around my throat. His fingers squeezed hard against my windpipe. Only a raspy, choking sound emanated from my mouth.

"It's a shame that when I take back my throne, the four of us cannot recreate that moment." Jax groaned, one hand around my throat while his fingers on the other dug deep into my hips as he thrust even harder.

Blackness tinged my vision, as I yanked on the hand around my throat. "I-I... I can't br-" I wheezed, coughing and spluttering loudly, when his fingers suddenly released their grip on my throat. Not that I had a moment to catch my breath before he forced my face onto Eleanor's breasts, encouraging me to suck them.

"Don't keep me waiting," Jax hissed; yanking on my hair once again, guiding me to the nipple of his choice. "Show me what you would do if Eleanor was Cassidy."

My mouth formed a perfect seal around her nipple, sucking as my tongue danced around it. Eleanor arched her back, squirming beneath me.

"Don't stop." Jax ordered, his breath coming in heavy pants.

The two shafts invaded my body with an increased ferocity, taking me over the edge and Eleanor along with me. We kissed and ground our hips together as we came. Both of us were still hungry for more. I pushed back against Jax, still buried deep inside my tight rosebud, wanting to feel his warm load to explode inside me.

That was when I felt something cold pressed into my palm and Jax's fingers clamped around my own.

"You must sacrifice something you love to prove your loyalty to me." He whispered in my ear, his voice cold and hard as he continued to thrust. I looked at the object in my hand. A silver dagger, but not just any dagger. It was my father's sacrificial blade.

I shook my head. "You *will* do it." Jax continued, his voice a rushed whisper in my ear. "You will not deny me, nor yourself, of that intense pleasure it will bring." I bit my lip, the darkness swirling in my body, taking over the control in my mind.

"Alyiah... do it. Now."

I looked at Eleanor. Her eyes were still closed as she reveled in the high of her orgasm. Her chest rising and falling with her ragged breaths.

"I-I c-can't." I whimpered, my body torn between disgust and desire. Jax drove his cock deeper and harder into my tight ass.

"Believe me, you will enjoy it," Jax murmured. "Together we will be unstoppable... I need your darkness Alyiah... it's the only way we can both get what we want."

Eleanor's eyes suddenly snapped open, fear and realization etched across her face. "Al.. please.. no-"

The vein in her throat pulsated; an attractive throb that was alluring. The darkness seized me, holding my humanity hostage in a chokehold. I could taste the fear as it oozed from her pores. I sensed her betrayal as her gaze locked onto me, wielding the blade before her.

This was my test; not only a choice between Eleanor and Jax, but between right and wrong - *good and evil*.

Suspended in time as it stretched on endlessly, I battled with the beast I had spent years trying to hide; fighting against the rush of adrenaline as it burst free from its restraints. *I do not want to be a monster*, I told myself as the blade quivered in my hands. *But I can no longer deny who I am - who I am destined to be.*

The compulsion overtook me. The darkness infiltrated my thoughts and took control of my body. My selfishness guided the razor-sharp blade across her throat. Sprays of crimson erupted as it sliced through the vein, splattering my exposed skin. The warmth of her life force on my naked flesh sent ripples along my body.

For a split second, my humanity resurfaced. My stomach heaved, and the blade slipped from my shaking hand. It landed on the flagstone floor with a deafening clatter. I felt my repulsion spiraling into regret and remorse, yet it was short-lived. The voices in my head told me it was too late; whispering my worst fear – *the demons have won.*

My inherited darkness smothered all doubts as if snuffing out lit candles. Power sizzled beneath my skin like an electrical current. Smearing the crimson liquid over my breasts, I rode the plastic shaft still buried deep inside me. So turned on by the thrill of taking a life, I was already teetering another orgasm. *My father was right. This is euphoric.*

Jax's hand pulled on my hair, twisting my head to face him. His eyes pierced mine as his load violently erupted deep inside me, clearly pleased by my choice.

"Does your darkness also crave my blood?" He asked, his voice clear of any emotion while his eyes glinted dangerously. I shook my head, leaning back into his body, enjoying the sensation of our unity as his hands let go of my hair and snaked around my waist. It was only when the curve of my spine felt his solid chest pressed against it that I realized with clarity that I had fallen into his trap. *This was the real test.* I had shown him what he had truly wanted to know; that even my monstrous side has a weakness.

TWENTY THREE

Once more, we were holed up in another dirty, run-down tavern on the northern border of Borjus which was the closest tavern to the port, while we waited out the storm. Time was against us, but I was a realist; if we left tonight as planned, at least half of us would perish in the treacherous conditions out at sea. *You didn't need to be a pirate to work that out.*

It was loud and rowdy inside the tavern. The noise drowned out the unrelenting rain that pelted against the single-pane windows and battered the roof overhead. There were too many people confined in such a small space. Trying to talk over one another, yet not hearing a single word. Only a constant hubbub of incoherent chatter.

These old stone walls were not built to hold fifty drunkards, let alone over a hundred drunk *pirates*. Toes were trodden on and steins of ale spilled as they tried to squeeze through the throngs of people.

It was only a matter of time before a brawl broke out. Fists swinging through the air, bodies slammed into tables and windows breaking. There is no better sound than breaking glass and shattering skulls... except *her* moans of pleasure. Right now, Cassidy and Logan were already fucking each other senseless, and there was nothing I could do other than let her pleasure wash through me. I welcomed the distraction of the fight, needing the adrenaline to override her orgasm that was building up once more. *If I can't fuck, I will fight.*

A circle formed in the heart of the tavern. Bodies everywhere obscured my view of whoever was the center of attention. My gaze caught Mad Morgan glaring out the window, into the stables and courtyard to the rear of the tavern. Under normal circumstances, a weary and tired trader would stop here; tying his horse inside the stable and shackling his cart in the courtyard. But not today, it housed the undead.

Rows and rows of them stood inhumanly still; commanded to wait for their orders to march on. Over the past several months, we had churned out hundreds of them; though sadly, not all of them had made it this far.

Demi's face flashed before my eyes; but I blocked the thought before it could develop. Losing her for a second time hurt just as much as the first. Anger blinded me. The need to punch someone, *anyone*, to unleash my pent-up frustrations. I was still no closer to finding Demi's murderer. There was no proof that tied him to the crime, apart from the fact that *Torvus* had fled.

I swung my elbows and cracked my fists into jaws, imaging them as the many faces of Torvus. *How dare he take her from me? After all the lengths I went to for her resurrection.* My knuckles connected square in the jaw of an unsuspecting victim.

Blood poured out of his mouth as he spat out three loose teeth. The man went to retaliate, but all it took was one look into my crazed eyes for him to back off. *I am unstoppable. Invincible. I will get my revenge. Torvus will pay for his crimes.*

Suddenly, a hushed silence fell over the crowd. Elbows nudged in rib cages, and excited whispers filled the room. I caught sight of her hard nipples poking through the fabric of her t-shirt. The pale see-through fabric was not the focus of my fellow pirates' attention; the beaten and bloody head, torn from his body by her bare hands, held their gaze.

I recognized the battered and bruised victim. The youthful, pimple-pocked face was known to me because he was not old enough to be here; still, he had chosen to join me. *Nate.* He had revealed that he too was seeking revenge for the wrongdoings of my brother, and had promised that he would do all he could to prove he was worthy to join us on my mission. He had mainly stayed in the shadows; scurrying behind us like the rats that feasted on the mess we left behind. *So why had Alyiah taken his life? What had he done to deserve this?*

The crowd parted when they noticed me approaching, the room deathly silent as they all listened to what I had to say with bated breath. I had a choice to make: pardon her crime and set a precedent for others to follow suit, or publicly punish her for her blatant disrespect and brutal crime against one of my men.

Alyiah never backed down. When the darkness consumed her, she never cowered in fear of me. But this was the fourth time in as little as seven weeks that she had killed someone. I could not let it slide so easily, not without just cause. But Nate was one of my men, someone who had survived the initial War. A young boy who had stood by and remained loyal to my cause.

"What the fuck Ally?" I hissed, grabbing her by the throat and squeezing tightly. "Tell me, what the fuck happened back there?"

"I didn't like the way he looked at me." She shrugged, dropping his head to the floor with a sickening thud. It rolled to a stop in front of its scrawny, lifeless body.

"Besides, he was no soldier... only a boy. A boy with a big mouth and a head full of hot air. *He* was a *liability*," Alyiah croaked under my five-finger necklace around her throat. "You should be thanking me."

I released my grip as Cassidy's climax ripped through my body and left me breathless. I could feel my balls throbbing, my cock threatening to erupt with the force of her pleasure. *Fuck.*

I dragged her out into the rain. Pushing her down to her knees and forcing open her mouth. My seed burst from the tip, spraying over her face before I had guided it fully into her mouth. Her eyes flickered up at me suspiciously.

"*That* was so fucking hot," I said. Although it was not a complete lie—the blood, the violence and the power turned me on. I would never reveal to anyone how deep my connection to Cassidy was; that everything she felt, I could feel. *It could be fatal should the wrong people find out.*

I felt her purr in appreciation as she swallowed the last of my cum. Her fingers buried deep into her pussy, uncaring that we were in the middle of a street in broad daylight. Unfazed by the rain drenching us and the wind whipping her hair in all directions.

"Tell me Alyiah, why Nate? What had he done?" I watched as she licked her lips and got to her feet. Grabbing at her hand, stopping her from savoring the taste of herself. "I want you to tell me what *really* happened."

Her eyes narrowed into slits, leaning forward, her breath hot against my earlobe. "He was trying to conspire against you. There are others who don't agree with your *unorthodox* approach to gathering an army. If you cut the plant at the root, you will stop the rot from spreading."

I released her hand, letting her suck on her fingers, tasting her own cum as a reward for her loyalty. For the first time in a long time, I felt as though at least I had one person I could trust with my life.

She may have thought the darkness would be her undoing, but to me, this unforgiving, unrelenting monster was the best thing to have happened to her, *to me*. Her hands wrapped around my cock and balls, teasing them back to life.

The darkness only craved two things: sex and blood.

I could live with that.

TWENTY FOUR

Jax

The ice cubes clinked against the empty glass as I slammed it down on the table. I had been here longer than I cared to admit, contemplating my future. *Drowning my sorrows.* I shifted on the wooden bar stool, trying to get in a more comfortable position.

This tavern was quiet, free from the whispered rumors of the latest gossip. Not that I needed to hear the news; I had felt it. Unsettling and worrisome; Cassidy was missing. I had not orchestrated such a command, so wherever she was or whoever had taken her was no friend to me. *Is this a decoy? Logan's plan to distract me or prevent my attack?*

I had been on a raid with the pirates when I felt her disappear; when our connection was abruptly severed. I had been accustomed to the dull ache in my chest. The sensation of our bond stretching as more time and space spanned between us. I could put up with it, knowing that it would disappear soon; once Cassidy was beside me, *or on top of me.* But now, there was nothing. It was worse. Feeling like a part of me was missing. Ruining all sense of concentration on anything else other than the void her absence left.

"Another," I muttered, sliding the glass forward in the bartender's direction. "In fact, just leave the bottle." I felt his glare judging me, wondering whether I could pay my way. I narrowed my eyes, ignoring the grotesque sight reflected in the mirror behind him.

This place is hideous. I chanced another glance at the dingy hovel I found myself in: The Velvet Witch. A small run-down tavern on the outside, and certainly not much better on the inside. Centuries old, made of mismatched stones covered in moss and lichen. Long, creeping vines obscured the old wooden sign fixed above the entrance.

The black wrought ironmongery had rusted in places, squeaking as the main doors opened to let a patron in or out. Both doors were badly scarred; each one bearing marks carved into it from flying axes or swinging swords. When I stepped into this hovel, I had very low expectations, yet it still surpassed them. The drab and dingy theme continued. Walls that were not made of grimy gray stone had been painted a different shade of shit. The floors were sticky, though I tried not to dwell on this too much; this was no ordinary tavern. It offered much more than just a pitcher of ale for its punters.

The bartender tried to keep the grimace from his face as his eyes caught the scene behind me. Quickly averting his gaze to the bottle in his hand. "You want me to leave this here?" he asked. My eyes narrowed, my stomach churning as the obese man sat in the booth grunted louder. The young blonde-haired witch kneeled before him, her mouth working his shaft.

"I'm surprised she could find it." The bartender sniggered, "underneath all that blubber." I sneered as I poured out a generous measure from the bottle of whiskey. I tried to keep my focus diverted elsewhere. The ice cubes in the glass, the grain of the wooden bar, *anything.*

I took a sip, feeling the golden liquid burn in my throat. Feeling the bile rise to meet it as the man groaned loudly.

"Uh- don't stop...fuck... so close." His voice was husky and primal.

"It's extra if you want me to swallow..." The witch purred, her wet lips smacking together as saliva drooled down her chin.

"I'll pay you triple if you stop," I snarled, spinning on my stool to face them. The witch was staring incredulously at me, her eyes pleading, hoping I was speaking the truth—to save her from *that* Hell. I reached into the inside breast pocket of the leather jacket. Pulling out a wedge of cash and thrusting it in her direction.

"I'm being serious."

Like cockroaches, the other witches came crawling out of the woodwork. They were all fixated on the stack of notes in my hand. Five of them; coming out from behind curtains and closed doors to the left hand side of the bar. It was obvious they had been waiting for their next patron to please. All eyes were on me—*I'm a walking, talking pot of gold.*

I smirked, opening my leather jacket, giving them a sniff of more notes stashed inside. As my father always said, *"Money is power."* But without the royal purse to fund my endeavors, I had to get creative, find a new way to get a lot of it quickly. That was where the pirates had fitted into my plan. I gained their trust by promising them bigger and better opportunities. As well as uncontested passage once I became King. *Promises I have no intention of keeping.*

"What the fuck?" The rotund man roared. Hastily shoving his manhood back into his pants as he watched the blonde move away from him without a backwards glance. Instead, she sauntered over to me, taking the bottle of whiskey from my hand and taking a big gulp.

"I need to wash away the taste of his dick," she whispered in my ear, her cleavage brushing against my arm. "I hope you don't mind."

The bartender grabbed the dissatisfied punter by the scruff of his collar. Roughly dragging him out onto the street. "Don't bother coming back!" he said as he slammed the doors shut, locking them before turning on his heel to face me. "So... you're Jax." The bartender's eyes studied me from head to toe.

"I am." I nodded, zipping up my jacket and perching once more on the barstool.

"You don't look much like a prince," he added as he drew up the stool beside me.

"Nor do you look like the High Warlock I am supposed to be meeting." A smug grin curling at the corner of my lips. "But as the only male working in this establishment; I can only assume that you are Darius."

As if needing to prove his magical prowess, two dazzling green balls of fire erupted from his palms. They grew more intense by the second.

"I could burn you where you stand," he hissed through gritted teeth. "But..." The flames slowly faded until they were gone completely. "You have something I want."

My smile grew wider; *my lucky ace.* It had been no secret that the witch who had cursed my sister with her ancient power had left behind a necklace. The witch claimed it was a talisman that could channel such sacred and powerful magic. Legend has it, now that my sister was dead, all the witch's powers had returned to the onyx set in the silver pendant.

Demi. There was a pang that resonated in my chest like a giant gong being struck hard. My anger flared. There were two people capable of getting that close to her; Alyiah and Torvus. The only thing that had shown Torvus' guilt was his sudden disappearance. Yet, I could not fathom what his motive was. *Why would he kill my sister? The beacon of hope for our futures?*

Another pang resonated in my chest. A stabbing that went deeper and felt sharper than before. It was quickly followed by a bubbling sensation that started in my nether regions. *It appears Cassidy has been found.* I scowled, my fury now at its crescendo.

"Jax... the amulet... is it true that it's still in the castle?"

My hands curled into tight fists at my side, my jaw set as I looked at Darius. "Yes." I hissed. "I know where it is, unlike my brother. Demi showed me where she hid it, should she ever need it."

"She should have used it before the battle." Darius chuckled.

My fist flew through the air, snapping a bone upon first contact. My other fist followed with a swift uppercut. *That should give you something to laugh about,* I thought. My anger sizzled as my breaths turned into pants. *I need that distraction now.*

"You will do what I say, warlock, you will support my cause and you will heed my orders," I said, standing before him with his hands covering his face. He nodded. Blood gurgled from his lips as he gasped in pain, while more trickled from between his hands over his eye.

"Good. Because that was nothing. You know what company I keep... failure to comply or attempt to deceive me will be severely punished."

The warlock cowered, noticing the witches' eyes watching his every move, he straightened his back; assuming a false bravado to keep his barbaric reputation. *The warlock could not lose face.*

Wincing as he spoke, he agreed to my terms. "But there are two conditions. First things first, before that scrawny ass of yours even touches that throne, you will hand over that amulet to me. *Only* me." He scowled, squaring up to me, the muscles in his jaw tense. "Second, if you want a girl, you pay like everyone else. No *special* favors."

I nodded, dumping the contents of my pockets on the bar. "Then I will have them all. Tonight, and every night, until I no longer require their services."

The blonde witch giggled, clinging to my arm. The others circled around me; each one removing items of clothing until they were completely naked. Darius' brow furrowed as he thumbed through the notes. I chuckled as I threw him a small canvas pouch bursting with gold coinage. "And that is for you to fuck off and give us some privacy." I added with a smirk.

Storming out to a chorus of giggles from the witches, he slammed the door closed. Not even giving us a backward glance. *Good.*

My eyes danced across every inch of their naked bodies; taking in each of their different aesthetics. The first was the sickly sweet blonde. The second a fiery redhead. The third was a witch whose hair looked as black as her soul. The fourth had candy-pink hair and porcelain white skin. The last, but in no way the least, looked like a tanned goddess. Her hair tumbled over her breasts in caramel waves. But the one who struck me the most was the doe-eyed, innocent looking brunette. *It will be easy to pretend she is Cassidy.*

The witches purred, their lips touching my exposed flesh as they peeled away at my layers of clothing. They made the right sounds, moved in the right way, but their eyes told a different story. I could see the fear that lurched behind each one of them. Their desperation and their compulsion to do as I commanded. *I want them to be afraid—fear is more powerful than respect.*

I tugged at the chain around the blonde's neck, noticing they all wore one. Made of a black metal chain with a heart-shaped padlock, looking more like a dog collar than a fashion statement. The necklace hissed beneath my touch, the metal red-hot against my flesh. I felt the burning sensation rise from my fingertips along my arm.

The pain was intense, like several electric shocks coursing through my body. "What the fuck is this?" I asked, holding on despite the pain, determined not to lose face.

"That is how he controls us," the blonde whimpered, shying away. "We can't... use our powers..."

Jerking my hand from the chain up to her face, clutching her chin tightly, I pulled her closer.

"Who? Darius?" I spat, my nails digging into the soft flesh of her cheeks. Her eyes widened as she frantically tried to blink away the tears that had formed. "What use are witches to me if you don't have your powers?"

"Only someone more powerful can remove Darius' spell..." The dark-haired girl muttered, "and it just so happens you are *friends* with the only person who is."

The blonde pressed her body closer to mine, gyrating her hips on my leg, leaving a glistening wet patch on my thigh. "Perhaps we could help you, if you *help us.*"

Cassidy's emotions were getting the better of me. Overwhelming and disorientating. Her relief at being in Logan's arms. The *pleasure* he was causing her. All of it made her momentarily forget the fear of *me* and of what was to come.

I was losing control. I could feel myself slipping.

Concentrate. You need the witches, I told myself. *I also need a distraction.*

I growled as I clutched a fistful of the brunette's hair, shoving her to her knees. "You know what to do." I barked. My other hand reaching for the blonde, rolling her nipple between my fingertips. Her sharp intake of breath made me shudder. My shaft was now uncomfortably hard.

I yanked on her hair, encouraging her to wrap her hands around my manhood; letting out a slight moan as she worked it in long, hard strokes.

I pulled even harder, my anger simmering beneath the surface. Not directed towards her but to who I wanted her to be - Cassidy. *She made me resort to this.* Looking at the brunette's innocent eyes, she was afraid of me. But she was too scared to break eye contact while her hands trembled around my shaft.

The tanned goddess crawled across the floor to join the brunette. I watched as her ass swayed from side to side as she approached, never once breaking eye contact. A devilish look glinted in her eyes, defiant—ambition. *She wants me to set her free.*

Sticking out her tongue, it trailed up my calf, along my inner thigh before running beneath my balls. A shiver rolled down my spine as her tongue lapped at them like a lollipop.

Cassidy's pleasure was still building inside me, but my own was soon to match hers. "Suck it," I demanded, forcing the brunette's lips open with the tip. As her mouth succumbed to the full length of it, the tanned goddess' mouth encompassed both balls. Licking and sucking until my breaths turned heavy.

I shut my eyes, imagining the scene before me differently. Pretending we were back at Alyiah's hut, that these mouths were hers and Cassidy's.

Soft moans garnered my attention as my eyes slowly flickered open. I could see nothing but the top of the pink-haired witch's head buried between the brunette's legs; her mouth devouring her from behind. Feeling the brunette's hot breath around my shaft as it stifled her moans. I pushed deep, feeling the tip hit the back of her throat.

The brunette's eyes snapped up at me as she gagged. Streams of mascara staining her cheeks as I clasped her head in place. *Try moaning now, bitch.*

My eyes settled on the fiery redhead, using my eyes to show her where she should be. It did not take her long to get the hint, throwing herself between the legs on the blonde, greedily lapping at her slit; her perky breasts bouncing as she devoured her with an intensity I had not seen from another woman before. *She loves it.*

Yet not as much as the black-haired girl. I spotted her sat on a table, legs spread wide, fucking herself with two fingers, her eyes full of lust and longing. *I will taste her first.* I let go of the blonde's nipple. She sighed as she buckled to her knees, forcing the red head's tongue deeper into her slit.

At the slightest movement, I felt all of their eyes locked on mine, wary of what I was about to do. I smirked; my power and dominance over these witches turned me on more than any acts they could perform. Their fear was almost tangible in the atmosphere, thrumming like an electrical pulse. They did not want to be here—to pander to strangers, to be used as a pet for their sexual needs. *They need me.*

A surge of energy buzzed through me, buffing my ego as their pathetic faces pleaded with me to help them.

"I didn't say fucking stop!" I barked, thrusting my hips deeper into the brunette's throat. Pushing deeper until her nose pressed up against my stomach. "Show me what you're worth."

I could feel Cassidy stirring inside, though I wasn't sure if she was watching or just happy *feeling* what I felt. I beckoned to the black soul, pulling her up onto the bar, leaning back so she could sit on my face. *If she is watching, she will get a good view.*

My arms outstretched on either side, I beckoned them all over. I could not see who was where, but I felt them. Two witches easing themselves down on my fingers. Stuffing their tight, wet cunts with as many of them that would fit. They left my thumbs free, so that I could rub their throbbing clits.

My hot breath danced over the black soul's smooth pussy. Making her moan out loud while another straddled my lap. I felt her warmth stretching around my cock, taking its full length to the hilt. A hot, wet mouth formed a seal around my balls. Sucking on one of them, warm saliva trickled down between them as the witch moved onto the other.

Where is the last witch? I thought. I looked to the side, watching as the tanned goddess climbed on top of the bar. Kneeling in front of the black soul. The goddess' teeth clamped on her nipples hard, making her scream out loud in pleasure. The pair of them shifted position until my face was directly beneath both of them.

I rolled my tongue from one to the other. A spark of electricity shot through them both. Seeing them arching their backs as their hands grabbed at one another's breasts. The pair of them kissed frantically, sloppy and wet, to muffle the sounds of their delight.

"Oh... Fuck... Logan...Don't... Stop!"

Hatred burned through my veins like fire, scorching a path towards my heart. Finding it engulfed in a blazing inferno that was Cassidy's climax. My resolve was slipping. I tried to focus on the six witches before me, but her pleasure was too much. My jealousy and longing for Cassidy taking over beyond redemption. *I need to block her. I want them to moan so loud they drown her out.*

The two witches on either hand rode my fingers in perfect synchrony. Moaning louder as I rubbed my thumbs in fast, frantic circles against their clits. The faster I moved my thumb, the harder they panted. *Good.* I thrust my hips up from the bar stool, the base of my shaft slamming against the witch. Within moments, the room filled with the loud slapping sound of skin against skin. *Better.*

I looked up at the two slits before my face, glistening in anticipation. Both of them rocked back and forth against my tongue, that danced between them. I felt one buckle as my mouth sucked on her clit, feeling her nectar trickle down my chin.

"My turn..." The tanned goddess purred, grinding her smooth slit against my eager mouth. I watched as her fingers drove into the sopping wet entrance on the black soul. She screamed as her juices erupted like a volcano. It sprayed over my face, drenching her inner thighs and dripped from the goddess' wrist.

Fuck. My body was overloaded with sensations; my pleasure and Cassidy's. Temporarily rendering me incapable of thinking about anything else but releasing my load. It was ready. My saliva-covered balls were full, ready to explode. *Oh fuck...*

I tried to move, but my body was pinned in place by them all.

"Get off." I roared, snatching my hands back. Roughly shoving the two witches away from my face so I could sit up. The pink-haired witch was still bouncing up and down on my cock, holding it hostage as it twitched violently. *I'm too fucking close.*

"Get the fuck off," I bellowed, digging my fingertips into her hips and throwing her furiously aside. In my peripheral vision, I saw her collapse on the floor, her body shaking as silent sobs escaped her. None of the other witches moved, frozen in their fear and anticipation of my next move.

Grabbing my cock in one hand, I directed it over the fiery redhead's face, forcing open her mouth with the other. Smirking as I noticed she was still riding her own fingers. The sopping wet sounds echoed in the otherwise silent room. My load erupted from my tip. More forceful and more powerful than I had been expecting. The combination of mine and Cassidy's orgasms ripped through my body. It sent my cum shooting out of my tip in thick white ropes. Smothering every inch of the redhead's freckled face. *Oh, fuck... that was close.*

Another tremor shook me to the core, different this time. Cassidy's anger, *no jealousy,* prickled inside my mind.

"Did you like the show?" I asked her silently, unable to hide my smugness or my breathlessness. *"I know you want me Cass, I know you hate the thought of anyone else riding my cock... tasting my cum..."*

"Fuck off Jax." She panted, trying and failing in her moment of vulnerability to close the connection.

That was when I saw her memory; one she was trying her hardest to conceal from me. I only caught snippets, but it was enough. *A black bird. The castle's courtyard. A shadow looming behind her as she reached for the door.*

Logan's panicked voice sliced through my mind as I saw him through her eyes. His dark brown eyes staring intensely into hers. *"Cass... you were taken... by a crow?"*

I hissed, my eyes glancing over to my clothes abandoned in a heap beside the bar. Hastily shoving them on, ignoring the hawk-like eyes of the witches stalking my every move. *Was it a crow?* I thought as I shoved on my boots without tying the laces. *Or was it a raven?* My hands fumbled at the lock on the entrance doors. *There was only one shifter I knew,* and I knew them *very* well. *Too well.*

The bitter cold air took my breath away as I burst through the doors, their iron hinges squealing in protest. Betrayal and hurt, seething in pure, unadulterated loathing. *Aliyah.*

"Fucking bitch," I muttered to myself as I tore through the streets towards the Inn we were staying in. Barricading my way through a couple, taking a midnight stroll hand-in-hand, as I neared. Desperately trying to cling onto the link with Cassidy. I needed to know what she knew, whether she had betrayed me. *Had she told them of my plans?*

I bit my clenched fist to stop myself from screaming as the last image imprinted on my mind. A black bird, covered in blood, a tuft of white-blonde hair clenched tightly in its talons.

I came to an abrupt halt as my mind pieced together the images like a puzzle. My eyes lingered on the dark and stillness beyond the Inn's windows.

"You will fucking pay for your deceit." I whispered, "and you will die an agonizing death."

TWENTY FIVE

Alyiah

Where the fuck is he? He said he would be back by now. I paced the dingy room, which was nothing more than a closet with a double bed pressed against the wall and a tiny sliver of a window. A small plastic clock nailed crudely to the wall ticked persistently. Each tick slowly drove me closer to the brink of insanity.

Four fucking hours I had been waiting for him; a lost puppy waiting for its master. *Only I am his pet crow.* The thought made me pause in my footsteps; my hand reaching for the handle on the only door in and out of this shithole. I twisted the knob, yanking on the door as I had a hundred times before; not yet learning my lesson when the door rattled on its hinges; refusing to budge.

Fuck. Jax knew I would not wait for him to return; he no longer trusted me with the darkness brewing within. He had taken the only key to this dump. It was also no coincidence why Jax had chosen this room; I had no escape. I knew where he was going; gathering with the pirates. Hoping to use the loot from yesterday's raid to put out a reward for the safe retrieval of *Cassidy*.

A lump formed in my throat at the thought of her. A part of me wished I had thought about it first; abducting her and destroying her. She was the only person who would stop me from having Jax and the future I had always dreamed of.

I strode over to the window, stretching on tiptoes and reaching for the clasp. It creaked open, the metal frame stiff and rusted. The gap was small; perhaps a little too small, *but I will make myself fit.*

Imagining my wings outstretching. Inhaling long, deep breaths, and fighting against the fear that flooded me each time I shifted forms. I reminded myself of all the techniques Eleanor had taught me over the years. My chest tightened. *Eleanor.*

The bile rose in my throat, flashes of her lifeless body flitted before my eyes: blood gushing from the slash across her neck. The elation and the overwhelming sense of chaos that flooded my body. The joy I felt as I watched her life force ebb away. The tantalizing energy that thrummed through my body as her blood dried on my skin. My orgasm was so intense it felt as if we were the sole occupants of the world; even time itself seemed to stand still.

I loathed the darkness for being when I felt most *alive.* When the world slept, I remained awake with nothing but disturbing thoughts to keep me company. Only Elanor knew how to soothe me; how to help me tame the demons trapped within my body. *Without her, I am lost.*

Jax had opened the floodgates, wanting all Hell to break loose, and having no intentions of redeeming my soul once he claimed the throne. *I am on my own.*

I contemplated those moments the darkness had overtaken me; recalling every moment as though I was watching someone else make the decisions. I was a puppet whose strings were being pulled by unseen hands. I wondered why I had allowed him to drag me into this mess; I could have said no. I should have refused to help him find my father. *I wish I had never met Jax Silverthorne.*

Ever since that day, he had been nothing but trouble. Making me doubt everything I thought I knew, longing for his attention the moment I heard he was back in Verancas. Even when he had proposed, it was like a dream had come true, although I knew the truth deep down. *He has no intention of making me Queen.*

My body began to shift into its bird form. *I had been stupid to think otherwise.*

In my jealous rage, I was going to shift so that I could spy on him. The demons taunting me, *"Jax doesn't want you because you are weak."*

"You're not good enough for someone like Jax."

"You will never replace Cassidy."

The unrelenting doubt made me dizzy; the knowledge that Jax had been with other women weighed heavy on my chest. *Why was I not enough for him?* Anger surged through my veins as I thought back to all the sacrifices I had made to please him. *But the more I gave him, the more he expected.*

Demi's resurrection would have been impossible without me. Jax's undead army would have remained a figment of his imagination. *I* took him to my father. *I* convinced him to help Jax's cause. *I* relinquished my humanity to his cause. *Yet it still was not enough.*

My father had a contingency plan should things go awry. He wanted me as his apprentice to carry on our dark family legacy, or he would refuse to help. *I had no choice. I just want to please Jax.*

My father demanded my full cooperation, respect, and loyalty to him. He would only continue to help Jax if I proved my loyalty to him over everyone - including Jax. When he gave the order to kill Demi and take a lock of her hair as proof, I had to obey. *Or die.*

I had fretted for weeks. Anxiously waiting for my father's signal as I stood by and let the monstrosity of Jax's plan unfold. It seemed Demi had become all he spoke about; how great the undead army would be. I should have been happy that for a brief period, he had stopped mentioning Cassidy. But I wasn't. Demi and his undead army kept Jax away from me.

So, when my father's command finally came through, I was all too willing to destroy Demi for good. I had gone to her room intending to kill her, my switchblade in hand, ready to plunge into her neck. It would be a lie to say I was not angry when I found out someone else had beaten me to it. Demi's body lay crumbled in the chair, a blade jutting out of her chest. Yet, I was also relieved. I did not have to face Jax with a guilty conscience, and could still fulfill my end of my father's deal. *I only had to hope the person who killed her was not also working for my father.*

The clock's chime snapped me back to reality. *What am I going to do?* What if Jax found out that I supposedly killed Demi? He would not take kindly to that level of betrayal. Even with the darkness inside me, I knew there were others like me out there in Xeyiera. *I was replaceable.*

Focusing harder on my shift, I knew what I had to do. I had to put myself first for a change. *I was going to leave now while I still could.* I was going to put as much distance between me and Jax as possible.

Long back feathers sprouted from my arms. I tumbled to my knees as I succumbed to the excruciating pain as bones shattered; the deafening sound of each one snapping and popping as they reformed into wings. Fierce determination raged through me; my self-preservation prevailed.

I clenched my hands, noticing how red and raw they were. *These hands have spilled too much innocent blood already.* I gritted my teeth, willing the rest of my body to change. I needed to get through this moment of weakness and vulnerability so that I could live to see another day. Even if it was seeing the rest of my days out in my raven form. *At least I would be free.*

The more I thought about it, the more the idea appealed to me. Soaring through the open sky, wings outstretched without a care in the world. The matters on the ground below are no longer of interest. I would live by my animal instincts; refusing to feel any human emotion. Sleep, eat and live as a raven and nothing more.

So entranced by this idea, I had not heard footsteps approaching the room. The door behind me crashed open, startling me. My wings were formed, but my body was still human. It only took one quick glance at his crazed eyes to know nothing good would come from this.

"So it was you," he hissed, his eyes darting from my wings to the open window. "All of it... was *you*."

His hands were around my throat, pinning me to the bed, my wings folded behind my back, unable to move. I struggled; trying to focus on shifting them back, but that only made him press down on my windpipe harder.

"Jax..." I tried to say. There was only one way I could tamper down his anger - sex. I knew I had to appease his brutal side, to turn his anger into lust. An unorthodox survival tactic, but it had worked in the past. "You're so fucking hot when you're angry."

A glint of silver caught the light; a blade clutched tightly in his other hand, raised above his head. *One downward thrust and that would be the end of me.* I ground my hips against his, feeling his shaft harden at the touch. "Don't you want to make Cassidy jealous?"

I felt the razor-sharp edge cut a little into my flesh. The sacrificial blade; the same one used to kill Eleanor, to murder all those babies.

The zipper of his pants ripped through the silence of the room. He already smelled of sex, of cheaply-perfumed whores. The thought of Jax fucking them repulsed me, made me jealous. *Is this what my life would become? Living in constant fight-or-flight mode?*

I bit down on my lip. I needed to play along. I felt his grip loosen slightly around my throat as he drove his cock deep inside my unwilling pussy. I recoiled, my body automatically flinching away from him. The blade pressed deeper.

"What the fuck did you say to her?" he scowled. "I know you betrayed me, Alyiah. I know you tried to warn her of my plans. But you are too late."

The sweet scent on his breath told me all that I needed to know. He had found the witches, had struck a seal with them, and walked away with a happy ending. *Witches did not need sexual favors, so what was really in it for them?*

I pulled him into a kiss as another distraction tactic. For a moment, Jax did not respond. *Shit, this will not work this time.* His hands stilled, his breathing shallow, when suddenly his lips crashed against mine. Hard, furious kisses. I could taste the other women on his tongue. I should have been used to it; this was not the first time. But back then I had been naïve. I was stupid to have ever believed Jax was true to his word. Now, I swallowed my pride, knowing everything Jax ever said to me was a load of shit.

"You can taste them, can't you?" He smirked, pulling away, his hips boring deep, bruising my own with his brutal thrusts. "You hate it as much as *Cassidy* does." He wiped his fingertip along the side of my neck, they came away slick with blood. his fingertip coming away with a trickle of blood. *My blood.* It may not have a lot, but it was enough to stir the darkness within. Jax smirked at my surprised expression, shoving his bloodied finger into my mouth.

I played along for a moment, ignoring the taste of my blood, forcing back my demons. But without warning, the darkness overcame me and I bit down on his finger hard. *He is not playing this time,* their voices whispered.

Jax yelped, yanking away his hand before I could bite the damn thing off. The blade fell from his other hand in shock. I scrambled beneath him, fleeing, wanting to transform one way or another to escape him.

Jax's hand reached for my ankle, clutching it in a vice-like grip. I screamed, trying to shake him off. His other hand slid the leather belt from around his waist. *No, no, no.* I jerked my leg, but even with my darkness inside, Jax was bigger, stronger. He looped the belt around my neck as he dragged me back towards him. *No!*

I kicked at Jax. My foot struck his solid stomach, but it only seemed to spur him on more. His grunts grew louder, more animalistic as he wrestled with me. Yanking on the belt, I gasped and choked as it tightened. Jax smiled sadistically, taking advantage of my open mouth. Forcing it to open wider with the tip of his shaft.

The taste of his cum, of me, of the other witch lingered on his skin; coaxing my jealousy to strike harder than before. *I never was not enough.* Back in Verancas, pleasure is pleasure. Love is love, regardless of gender. We did not believe in *mates*, or at least I never, until I met Jax. What Eleanor and I had was special, as close to a monogamous relationship as we would ever have. But Jax *believed*. He pined for his soulmate, knowing she had made her choice - and it was not him. *He could choose another mate, but he refused. I would give him a reason to choose me.*

The darkness simmered. This was my last chance to diffuse the situation. I ran my tongue along the length of it. Choking myself further as I moved my head forward, enveloping his full length in my mouth; drawing in my cheeks and tucking in my teeth, I worked his solid cock in quick, hard bursts, the way he always liked it. My eyes never left his. I silently prayed. *Please, let this work. I will give him what he desires most: control.*

My saliva trickled down my chin, gagging as the head of his shaft brushed the back of my throat; twitching against my tongue as he thrust his hips, fucking my mouth. I heard his grunts and felt his grip loosen on the belt as his hot seed shot down the back of my throat; struggling to swallow it all, globules escaped my lips when he withdrew. His eyes were mesmerized by them as they trickled down my chin and onto my cleavage.

"Lick it up," he demanded, grabbing my breast in one hand and forcing my head to bend unnaturally towards it. My neck clicked and my chin pressed against my collarbone. A shooting pain ran along the base of my skull and down my spine. Yet I continued to obey, my darkness biding its time, waiting for another perfect moment. My tongue swirled around in the pool of his cum to the sound of his sinister chuckle.

Stupidly, I thought that was the end; I had been let off with a warning. I relaxed as he backed away from the bed. But I was wrong. His firm hands pushed me backwards to the bed, rolling me over. He grabbed my waist and pulled my ass up into the air. His fingers bore into my fleshy hips.

"You're going to be a good girl and take it dry." He groaned as he forced the head of his cock between my ass cheeks, prying open my tight rosebud entrance. I winced, feeling it stretch and tear.

I surrendered to him, biting on the bedding to stifle my cries. With each whimper that escaped my lips, he sunk an extra inch deeper. Impaling me with every inch of himself as his thighs slapped against the flesh of my ass cheeks.

Despite my fear, or perhaps because of it, I enjoyed it. The darkness purring inside me like a kitten, getting one of its two fundamental desires - sex. *Next would be blood.* I shut the thoughts from my mind, feeling my body slowly relax. My pain, his pleasure. *Our* pleasure.

The harder he thrust, the closer to the precipice of climax I came. The fire inside me was ablaze with lust and desire, erasing all my thoughts of escaping. Jax was broken, like I was when Eleanor had found me. *I can fix him.*

I crumpled to the bed before my orgasm could take hold. Jax's sudden withdrawal irked me. *I was so fucking close.*

Jax's smug grin reflected off the discarded blade beside my face. "I'll be right back."

TWENTY SIX

Cassidy

Logan's dark eyes bore into mine, intense and full of love; unable to contain his smile even as his lips crashed against mine. Our heads sinking deeper into the long grass.

"Cass... I'm so glad you're safe... that you're *here.*"

His hands slid under my nightdress, which was still damp from falling in the snow. I tried to push the image aside, blocking my thoughts from Logan. *There would be a time and a place but this is not it.* I gasped as his fingers traced along my thighs. I bit down on my bottom lip to stifle my moan as his fingertips eased their way inside me, while his thumb brushed over my clit.

Logan used his knees to part my legs wider. His lips wandered all over my body: down my neck, along my collarbone, and across my cleavage. Teasing each nipple underneath my silk bodice until they stood like two hard bullets. My fingers dug into the grass, clutching fistfuls of it. My need and lust blossomed like the wildflowers that surrounded us.

I gazed up at the sky, my eyes scanning for any sign of Torvus in his crow form. *Would I ever see him again?*

I tried to clear my head from thoughts of him as my breathing grew heavier. Logan's fingers become more frantic as they thrust deep into my core. *Have I doomed us all?*

Logan suddenly stopped, his eyes locked onto mine. For a split second, I thought my charade had slipped, that Logan had seen or heard my thoughts. When suddenly, his smile widened as he pulled me on top of him; feeling his hard bulge pressing firmly against my crotch.

"Cass, you have *no idea* how much I was worried about you." He murmured, his breath hot against my ear as he craned his neck up to reach me. A smile tugged at the corners of his lips as I instinctively moved my hips against his. My whole body was on fire.

"Your throne awaits you." He chuckled, sliding himself lower, until his face was in line with my smooth mound. "Your King demands you sit on it at once."

That is an order I will never refuse.

Pinning his head between my slick thighs, Logan's magical tongue went to work. My moans echoed, but unlike back at the castle, I was not fearful of being overhead. Here at the lake, it was only us. *Our* sacred spot. The only place we could forget the burden of our positions; forget our responsibilities. We could just be lovers, wanting nothing more than one another.

I knew I had made the right choice. All those years ago, the stranger who had disturbed the secrecy of the lake had also staked a claim on my heart. My only regret was not choosing him sooner; being too afraid to upset or anger Jax. *I could have prevented the war...*

My body tensed, recognizing Jax's presence instantly. I tried to ignore him, to focus on Logan and only Logan, but Jax had other ideas. Flooding my body with his pleasure. His vision flooded my own, so that I was now gazing down upon several girls. *Witches*, even. Each one performing a sexual act of some sort upon him.

I thought of Alyiah, but I could not see her there. *Where was she?*

"She is not important," he snapped.

"Cass?" Logan whispered, "Are you ok?"

I nodded my head, positioning myself over the tip of his shaft, slowly lowering myself down onto him. "I am fine," I replied, giving him a small kiss on the lips. "I love you, my King."

Jax's anger ripped through my body, thrumming like a thousand angry bees as I ignored him. Instead, focusing solely on riding Logan, hard and fast. I brought myself to another orgasm within moments. It was not enough; Jax retaliated, determined to make me jealous.

"It's working, isn't it?"

I shook my head, trying to push away the image of the two girls above him. His body was alive with excitement of dominance and power, enjoying his pleasure as if I were him.

My breath clogged my throat. Logan's hands gripped my waist, slamming me down and causing my breasts to bounce wildly. The thin straps of my dress barely contain them from spilling out of the dress. The echo of my moans floated on the breeze.

My muscles spasmed and my walls held his shaft firm while my climax claimed my body entirely. Thousands of fireworks exploding across my skin as I let out a cry of sheer bliss. Our heavy breaths panted in unison as I felt his seed fill my core. My body trembled as it crumpled down onto his; soaking in the warmth of his skin.

"Cass," Logan said after a few moments of enjoying the tranquility of the moment. "Where have you been?"

A shadow in the bushes caught my attention. My eyes darted from Logan to the spot I stood in on the other side of the lake. I blinked several times; trying to make out who the shadowy figure was.

I saw it shake its head; seeing the robe sway as it paced the lake's edge. *Was that one of the Elders?* My eyes followed its every movement. *Were we being watched the whole time?*

Logan's lips fluttered against my cheek, snapping my attention back to him. I noticed his brow knit together with concern as his eyes scanned the circumference of the lake.

"Cass, what are you looking at?"

It was my turn to frown as my eyes darted from his face back to the other side of the lake. The figure was gone. I had only looked away for a split second, but the grassy verge was empty. No sign that anyone had been there at all.

A shiver ran down my spine, leaving goosebumps in its wake. I no longer felt safe; our sacred place had lost its tranquility and secrecy. "Did you not see him?" I asked, "someone was there." I pointed to where the figure had been pacing. "I think it was one of the Elders."

Logan's fingertips brushed the side of my face as his eyes studied my face. "Cass... no one was there."

Taking a few deep breaths to steady my nerves, I knew what I had to do, what I *should* do. After all, he was my husband, my soulmate. Logan and Felix were all I wanted to protect. *Logan's security will fail if he does not know everything.*

I opened my mind to him. Instantly Logan spoke. "Cass... you were taken... by a bird?"

Nodding slowly, I let my memories flood into his mind.

"That's not even the craziest part," I muttered, focusing on the view from the top of Mount Hejha. I showed him the skull I tripped over and the werewolf that attacked us.

"Why didn't you tell me about what Jax was doing?" I added, my eyes filling with tears as they landed on the bag dumped a few feet away from us. "Why did you keep it from me?"

Logan was silent for a few moments, his thoughts shrouded by my memories as he tried to process it all. "I wanted to keep you safe," he replied, his voice feeble and unconvincing.

"*That is a bullshit excuse.*" I replied through our telepathic connection. Logan remained silent.

A sigh escaped my lips as I dragged the bag over to me, retrieving the only item that was inside: the wooden box. My heart raced as I lifted the lid to check on the contents.

"Tell me the truth, Logan." I whispered, my fingers tracing the glass of the vials before snapping the lid shut. "I *deserve* to know the truth..."

"You're right," he sighed, placing his hand on top of my own and his metal one over the lid of the box. "I know about your connection with Jax... I know he has contacted you. I have withheld information from you because... I don't want it going back to my brother."

"I would never!" I gasped, horrified. "I would never do anything to put you or Felix in more danger! I would rather drink this..." Logan silenced me.

"I know you wouldn't *willingly*, but I know Jax will manipulate you, will take what he can from whoever he can, until he gets what he wants," he said, his eyes sweeping over my face. "But I am not letting him get you."

A single tear rolled down my face, Logan's metal limb quickly wiped it away. "He *will* have to kill me to get to you..."

My gaze dropped to the wooden box, our intertwined fingers holding the lid closed. "We will keep these safe," he whispered, "but I promise it won't come to that."

"But... what about my dreams... Torvus' visions?"

"Cass... I believe we make our own Fate. *You* chose me, *you* changed my fate," he whispered, his lips brushing against my forehead. "I would have died on that battlefield..."

My finger trembled as I held it against his lips. Images of Logan lying on the battlefield, his life slipping away. Blood pumping from his fatal dismemberment. Once again, I was consumed by the feeling of helplessness. My own healing abilities were not enough to save him.

"I love you, Logan." I whimpered, moving my fingers down his angled jaw, tilting his lips up to mine. "But I can't do what Torvus proposed..."

Logan's fingers squeezed mine, staring at me with glassy eyes. "I would never ask you to."

TWENTY SEVEN

Flynn

Time was not on our side. The persistent ticking of the clock was a constant reminder that Cassidy had been gone too long. The hands on the clock, a poignant announcement that I had less than fifteen minutes until my duty would start; when I would stand vigil outside Felix's room to relieve Esan of his position. Logan had insisted on going alone in his search for Cassidy.

"That is not a wise decision." I told him, but he shrugged it off and barked strict orders for Esan and I to remain at the castle. Neither one of us was to let Prince Felix out of our sight. He only trusted us to watch and protect his son, the heir to the throne.

Esan had volunteered for the first sitting, but I did not know how to fill my time. Too anxious about both of their safety to put my mind to do anything. Even neglecting my husband as I fretted, walking back and forth in front of the arch window in our room. Glancing out now and then, hoping I could see one of them. *Cassidy would never forgive me if something happened to him.*

Jace's eyes watched me pace the same spot. "You will wear a hole in that floor," he said, trying to make light of the situation. His eyes were trained on me like a hawk, listening and feeling my every thought and emotion. "Flynn... you are obeying a direct order."

He walked over to me. His firm hands stopped me in my tracks as he held me in front of him. "Logan is a fierce warrior, a fighter when he needs to be."

"He hasn't been going to his training sessions; he hasn't even tried the new attachment Cassidy's father made him," I spluttered; my eyes cast out onto the horizon. The image of the razor-sharp spike Cassidy's dad forged over a year ago, played in my mind as it remained untouched in the armory.

"Jace, he hasn't even held a sword since..." My shoulders sagged. "I should have done more to stop him."

I felt the warmth emanate from his skin as he embraced me. "There was nothing you could have said or done that would have stopped him. Nor could you have gone against his commands." Jace's breath was warm against my neck. "Logan would go to Hell and back for Cassidy,"

He tilted my face up to his. "I know he would rather die in his search for her than stuck here waiting for news."

"How do you know that?" I asked him, lifting his chin so that I could see into his eyes.

"Because that's what I would do if you were the one missing."

The force of his kiss took my breath away, pinning me up against the glass window. "I would leave no stone unturned... no valley left untouched... no shadow unexplored," he added between kisses. His fingers expertly unbuttoned my shirt, giving him a path of exposed flesh to grace with his lips.

As his kisses moved south of my torso, my rigid shaft brushed against his body. It sent a tremor of anticipation through me. *I would do the same too.*

My heart pummeled hard in my chest. My lust scorched through my veins as I saw him on his knees before me; staring into his eyes as he looked up at mine while unfastening the zipper of my pants. My rigid shaft throbbed against the zipper, desperate for freedom. I needed to feel his lips around it, to take me to bliss, no matter how temporary it may be.

I held my breath in anticipation as Jace rolled down the waistband of my pants. Easing my boxers down with them until they both pooled around my ankles. My lungs were on fire. I fought against the instinctive nature to breathe, to moan, to make any noise at all; fearing that we would be overheard. Even after the abolishment of Clause 4a, I still feared our intimacy being overheard.

Jace's tongue worked its way over my balls. His mouth cupped each one, taking his sweet time, enjoying every moment. My throbbing shaft twitched with jealousy; it wanted some attention too.

"Relax, boo." Jace whispered. His breath was hot against my member while his lips brushed against the purple engorged tip. I felt his firm grip on my thighs; slowly working his fingers in small circular movements to ease my tense muscles.

It was easier to relax as Jace's mouth sealed around my shaft, slowly taking it deeper. Only when my full length was encompassed in his warm, wet mouth could I push my thoughts of Cassidy to the back of my mind; gripping onto the window ledge and allowing myself to not think of anything, but to simply *feel*.

A tingling sensation rippled through my body. Jace was the master of my desires, making quick work of taking me to the precipice of my climax. I moaned. It came out louder than intended, reverberating off the stone walls. I looked around, panicked, but I had no time to wait to see if anyone heard me.

My shaft spasmed, my hands automatically reaching for him. Bracing his head in position as wave after wave of my hot cum shot down his throat. Each wave was stronger and more powerful than the last. The beautiful harmony of my moans and his soft gagging fell into perfect synchrony. I refused to let him pull away until he swallowed every last drop. *Fuck, he is so good.*

"Flynn... Oh! *Shit.* "Logan's voice snapped me out of my orgasmic high. My eyes darted to the door, my body frozen as my seed still pumped from my shaft into my husband's mouth. But it was not just the King of Eyre staring at me, but his wife, the Queen, too. *Cassidy.*

I was not sure what emotion to feel first; embarrassment or relief. My orgasm shuddered through my body as I stared at them both. Unable to move.

Cassidy's cheeks blushed a deep scarlet, her gaze averted to the floor. "Um, I... uhh... sorry," she murmured before disappearing away from the door. Her hand tugged at Logan's arm, who was still standing there, staring. Walking in on us had shocked him, but he was not appalled.

"Man, I'm sorry. I should have knocked." Logan blushed. It was hard to tell whether he was still watching because he was still in shock or was he a little *curious?* We were both aware of Cassidy's tryst with Jax in Verancas. We knew Cassidy was no stranger to experimentation.

Logan's eyes caught mine, his face flushed a deep scarlet. Jace chuckled as he wiped at the corners of his mouth with the back of his hand. His eyes twinkled with humor as I frantically pulled up my pants and readjusted my manhood. He averted his gaze the moment he realised it was rock solid once more.

"Um... I should go..." Logan mumbled as he pulled the door closed. I listened to the sound of his rushed footsteps echo in the hall, unmoving from my position until they faded into the distance.

"Has the thought of our handsome king watching you cum turned you on?" Jace purred in our mental link, his face nuzzled into my neck. His mouth planting kisses along my jaw while his hands shoved mine down to his crotch. The bulge beneath my hands throbbed as Jace's smirk widened. *"Me too."*

A shudder shook my body, filling me with lust. I was torn between my selfish desire and my need of reassurance that Cassidy was here, safe and unharmed. I reached out to her, yet refusing to remove my hand from Jace's crotch. Indecisiveness eating me from the inside out.

I felt her voice echo in my mind, even her mental voice could not hide her embarrassment. *"Flynn, I'm...s-sorry! We just—we wanted to tell you ... never mind"*

"Cass, just knock next time." I said, trying to make light of the awkwardness, trying to keep my voice light-hearted. hearing her voice and knowing she was safe. *"Tell me, what the hell happened? Where the fuck were you?"*

"I'll ... I'll explain later... when you're less, um, busy."

"I will hold you to that." I felt the anxiety and fear slowly fade from my mind. The dark thoughts of never seeing her again vanishing like smoke in the wind. The sensation of Jace's warm body pressing against mine once more while his lips danced over my skin.

My hands slipped beneath the waistband of his shorts, Jace took a deep breath before nipping lightly at my neck. My eyes locked onto his as my other hand cupped his chin, watching his lips form a seductive grin. I leaned in to kiss him, dragging his bottom lip between my teeth. "Now, it's my turn."

TWENTY EIGHT

Logan

Tendrils of brown hair, floating in the wind. Her brown eyes twinkled as she laughed. Fascinated by her plump lips clamping down on the watermelon slice; I watched the juice trickle down her chin, resisting the urge to reach over and wipe it off. The urge to replace that watermelon with my lips, to kiss her until our lips were sore and bruised, overtook me. Together we rolled around in the long grass; forgetting the rest of the world existed.

It's funny how something as innocent as eating a piece of fruit had become one of my sexiest memories of her. I knew back then I loved her. That I would do anything for her. Cassidy was the most beautiful woman in the whole of Xeyiera, *and she's mine.*

There were no words to describe my elation when I saw her staring back at me from across the lake. The sheer happiness that consumed me when I held her again in my arms. *I'm never letting Cassidy out of my sight.*

I let her guide me through the labyrinthine corridors of the castle. Our fingers interlocked. Joy filled my heart as memories played through my mind like a cinematic reel. Feeling Cassidy stop now and then to kiss me, her plump lips curled into a smile as her memories played out too.

I was so caught up in the moment that I did not realize what we had stumbled into. Cassidy's hand slid from mine. A flood of embarrassed and arousing thoughts flooded my mind. I felt my cheeks burn as I stared at the two men before me.

Never had the thought of same-sex relationships turned me on before. I was not curious. I knew what I wanted, *who* I wanted. As long as I had Cassidy, I was content. *So why did seeing Flynn and Jace affect me so much?*

One moment her hand was outstretched to me, trying to pull me away. The next, the sliver of her dress whipped at her ankles as she disappeared around the corner; her thoughts blocked from me once more while she ran ahead. I quickened my pace to catch up with her, my hands clutching at her waist the moment she was within reach. Breathless, I turned her around to stare at her. "Cass... what was *that* about?"

A deep crimson spread across her cheeks, her gaze averted to the floor. It was then that I realized the arousal was not mine, but *hers*.

"I-I..." she murmured, refusing to look at me. *"It was just so... natural,"* her mental voice whimpered. *"It reminded me of... us."*

My hand ran through her hair, pulling her into a kiss. Deep and sensual. *"I mean... It was not so much the act but their love for one another. I know you would never... um... do anything like that,"* she added.

I felt Cassidy pull away from me once more, scurrying on ahead in her embarrassment as she headed to our son's room. There was something else that had aroused her, something she refused to reveal to me.

We walked on in silence, feeling it become awkward and oppressive as we passed Jax's old bedroom. Images of her time with Jax sprung into my mind before she could block them, her eyes glancing at me guiltily. In that moment, she opened her mind fully to me, revealing her most recent connection with Jax.

Women surrounded him, pinning him down as they thrashed against his mouth and his fingers. I could feel his climax, watching on as he covered one woman with his load. I was speechless. The scene was so *brutal*, barbaric and borderline disrespectful. I never knew something like that would rile Cassidy like it did.

Cassidy stilled as I drew her closer to me, holding her hips against mine. The way she squirmed in her lust made my cock rise. My lips locked onto hers. A kiss so passionate and driven by a carnal desire that it led to me pin her against his door. My member was rock solid as it pressed against her, hoisting her leg around my waist to get even closer to her. I wanted her now more than ever.

Cassidy broke the kiss, breathless with eyes wild with lust. "I'm sorry... I know I shouldn't... Logan, I only want to be with you..."

I held her face cupped in my hands. I could feel her shame and apprehension. Her thoughts swirled in my mind, worrying that I would be angry or upset. I chuckled lightly as my thumbs stroked her cheeks. "Cass, I know you do."

"You're not *jealous*?" she whispered, biting her bottom lip.

"Would it turn you on even more if I was?" I said, pressing my bulge against her groin. The fire within her feeling the fire rise like a raging inferno. Her sharp intake of breath and mischievous twinkle in her eyes made my shaft even more rigid. She bit her lip and nodded.

My arms crushed her body to mine. Fierce, possessive, demanding. "*I want you. Now.*" My mental voice told her as the scent of our sex radiated from her skin. The damp-grassy fragrance from the lake still lingering on her clothes.

I opened my mouth to speak, her teeth grazing over my bottom lip. "Of course, it makes me crazily jealous and fiercely possessive." My hands dropped to her breasts, teasing her hard nipples between my fingertips. "Though you are sexy when you are so worked up."

My breath was hot against her ear. "I am the lucky one." I bit down gently on her earlobe. "All I need, all I *want...* is *you.* Always."

A moan escaped her lips and reverberated through the empty corridor. Her back arched away from the door while her hands explored my body; enjoying the feel of my prominent bulge protesting against the tight fabric of my pants beneath her palm.

We lost ourselves as we kissed, disregarding our location; so absorbed in one another that neither of us heard footsteps approach.

A male voice startled us as he cleared his throat. Both of us pulled away, disheveled, our chests heaving as we panted heavily. "My King... My Queen..." One of my personal guards, Xavier, smirked as he addressed us, sliding his sword back into its sheath attached around his waist. "It's nice to see you both safe and *well.* But I must insist you keep your *antics* to private quarters."

I started chuckling, reluctantly disentangling myself from Cassidy. "What is with the sword? Did you mistake us for promiscuous intruders?" I joked.

"I-uh.. well, I wasn't expecting to find the two of you..." He replied; his cockiness suddenly diminishing. "I was actually on my way to retrieve Flynn so he can relieve Asan from his post as you commanded..."

"That is no longer necessary." I quipped, glancing over at Cassidy. "Besides, Flynn is a little *busy* at the moment." I smirked as Cassidy's cheeks blossomed into a deep scarlet while Xavier baulked. It was his turn to be embarrassed, shuffling his feet on the ground, his eyes diverted.

"Give over Xavier, you're the father of how many children now? Five? Each one with a different mother..."

"A sixth is on the way... but what can I say? I'm a *breeder.*"

Cassidy brushed past us hastily, eager to get to Felix's room, her thoughts a tangled web of sex and orgasms. I smirked as her innocent thoughts tried to imagine what a breeder got up to. *"I can show you if you'd like"* I smirked, seeing her step falter as my mental voice echoed in her mind.

I raced up to her, not giving the guard a second thought. Instantly nuzzling her neck, desperate to cling to her arousal for a little while longer.

"Later... I promise," she said, turning around to face me, the lust in her eyes now only smoldering embers. "I *need* to see Felix," she added.

The moment she stood outside our son's room, her thoughts immediately changed; growing sinister and macabre. Flashbacks from her dreams danced before her eyes, instantly erasing all other thoughts. I watched as she took hold of the brass doorknob with a trembling hand and twisted while her heart thumped deafeningly in her ears.

She took three tentative steps into the dark room beyond. Her head moved side to side as her eyes adjusted to the dim lighting; her shoulders sagging in relief at the sight of Felix sleeping in his cot. His room was as immaculate as it had been when she had left. Not a stray toy out of place. *Nor a single drop of blood in sight.*

Rushing to his crib, her gaze never left the tuft of dark brown hair, stark against his pale blue bedding. For almost a day, he had been wailing and crying for his mom. But now that she was here, he was completely unaware of her presence.

I could see her battling against the vision and the compulsion to scoop him up into her arms as she leaned over the crib, silently watching as the blanket rose and fell with each breath. Her fingers trembled as she traced every line on his sleeping face.

"What did Torvus say about these visions, Cass?" I asked softly, my arm wrapping around her waist as I stood beside her.

"There is a way for them to change." She whispered, her voice barely audible. "but, I—I don't think I can do it..." Her shoulders shook as she sobbed, "I don't want anything to happen to him... or you... but- but..."

I took a deep breath, wrapping both arms around her, drawing her head to my chest, and allowing her to cry freely. It was hard to stomach the pain she was feeling. The guilt and fear; ready to explode at any moment. She wanted to be free of her bond with Jax, but felt a warped sense of loyalty to him despite his evil deeds.

"I want to hate him," she continued, "I don't want to feel this way."

"I know," I soothed, kissing the top of her head; inhaling the scent of her. "It won't come to that-"

"But while he is out there... while he is *alive*. Nothing will ever change. He wants everything you have... it's clear he won't stop until he does." Cassidy tilted her face up towards me. "We can't let him win, Logan..."

"We won't," I replied, kissing those soft, plump lips. "I promise." A fierce determination shot through me. The possessive and territorial side of me unleashed, *and that is a promise I will not break.*

I felt Cassidy's head rest against my shoulder, her silent sobs quaking through her body. Tears cascading down her face freely, after she had given up trying to swipe them away with the sleeve of her robe.

"I can't live in a world without you in it..." She sniffed, her glassy eyes looking up at mine. "I wouldn't even want to try."

The sun was setting, casting deep reds and purple stripes across the tops of the trees. They reflected vibrantly on the lake's surface like watercolors on canvas. We had never been there together, the three of us. The lake had always been *ours*—just Cassidy and I.

"We should show Felix the lake." Cassidy had said earlier, as we watched over his crib. *"I think he would love it there."*

We had waited for over an hour for him to rise. The two of us, in comfortable silence, not needing to speak to enjoy each other's company. There was no denying Felix's happiness the moment his eyes found his mother. *Everything was right with the world once more.*

As we walked to the lake, hand in hand and Felix in his stroller, Cassidy's words echoed through my mind. *"I can't live in a world without you in it... I wouldn't even want to try."* As selfish as it sounded, those words appeased me. It solidified my belief that what we had was *real*–deeper than any soulmate bond—true love. Yet the thought of what was to come clouded my happiness. I stared at the clumpy metal limb that hung limply at my side. *How am I supposed to protect us?*

Laughter split through the air, melodic and in harmony, as Cassidy chased Felix through the long grass. Scooping him up into his arms as if he were weightless when he got too close to the edge of the lake.

I watched in silence, sitting on a nearby tree root that protruded out of the ground. *I wish every day could be like this. I wish my brother wasn't intent on trying to ruin it.*

A loud squawk startled us all, as a huge black mass swooped across the lake. Eventually, coming to a stop to perch on a branch nearby, where it continued to squawk several more times.

"Bird... bird..." Felix smiled, pointing at it. The crow's beady eyes followed Felix's every move. I did not like the way it was watching him, or *us,* almost like that of a predator stalking its prey. Cassidy didn't like it either.

"Torvus, is that you?" she whispered, moving closer. "If it is, please show yourself in human form."

The bird didn't move, didn't even flinch. "Torvus..." she said again, moving closer, opening her mouth to say something else. Placing herself between the bird and Felix. He grumbled, squirming from behind her trying to see this majestic bird. Wanting to touch the iridescent feathers as they rustled in the late evening breeze. There was something different about this bird, I noted. I recalled her memory of the crow she had seen moments before her kidnapping. *This is not the same bird.*

Before us sat a bigger, more *powerful* bird. With a tail shaped more like a fan. Its black eyes focused on the three of us, completely devoid of any expression. *"That is not the same bird, Cass."* I tried to warn her.

That is not a crow. It's a raven.

In every myth book and legend, ravens and crows were mysterious creatures. Associated with magic and forbearing visions. Very few people could distinguish between the two. Even less knew the actual difference between the breeds.

Ravens were created to deceive humans; to lull them into a false sense of security. They were creatures derived from the underworld; fashioned by the Devil himself.

I threw myself at them just as the raven's wings outstretched, launching itself at Cassidy's face. Its talons would have struck her had I not jumped in the way. Gouging three long slashes along my back. It squawked loudly and flapped its wings frantically as it took flight once more. *A shifter—and a powerful one at that.*

TWENTY NINE

Cassidy

Blood trickled from his wounds and his face contorted in pain as he sank to his knees before me. The bird was now invisible against the blanket of darkness that had suddenly fallen.

"Let me heal you," I whimpered, kneeling beside him and placing my right hand on his solid chest; feeling his muscles ripple beneath my fingertips as he tried to steady his breaths. Stubbornly, he shook his head, as he tried to dab at the wounds with his fingertips. "Logan," I sighed, taking the shirt from him and lightly holding it to staunch the blood flow. "I am a healer. Let me help you."

My hands felt hot as they radiated light from my palms, sinking into his chest and disappearing beneath his skin. It glowed through his veins as it moved inside his body, finding the quickest path to his injuries. He scowled, squirming not out of discomfort, but reluctance.

Ever since the troll attack, Logan had been hesitant to let me use my healing abilities, especially on him. I had used too much energy too quickly in my rush to heal Flynn; making rash decisions while blinded by fear. I had not been trained to heal such extensive wounds.

"Stop being difficult," I murmured, feeling the warmth radiating across his skin from beneath his shirt. I removed it, watching as the slices of his flesh knitted together. Only a faint white line marked the location of his wound. Within a few minutes, that too had disappeared.

"Logan, I love you, but you really are as stubborn as old boots." I smiled once the final wound had closed. He rolled his shoulders back and tilted his neck from side to side. I stared in fascination as the muscles rippled with every movement.

I felt him turn to face me. "It's not stubbornness, Cass..." he sighed, his gaze dropping to the metallic hand propping him up. "It's just... sometimes, I just feel so weak and useless."

My arms wrapped around him so fast it caught him off guard, both of us tumbling into the long grass. "You are *not* weak," I hushed, my lips brushing against his.

"Says the one pinning me down." He smirked.

"Only because you love it when I'm on top," I teased, my teeth grazing against his lower lip.

"Mama... dada look-" Felix's squeaky voice instantly drew my attention. He was standing on the edge of the lake, leaning over to stare at his reflection. "Shiny... water-"

"Felix... come away from the edge," I called, getting to my feet, trying not to alarm him.

"I see.. wanna see." He mumbled, his hands reaching out to something in the centre center lake.

It all happened in slow motion. Felix took little steps deeper into the lake, first the water covered his ankles and then his knees. When suddenly he fell, completely disappearing from sight into the murky depths below the surface.

I screamed. My feet battered the ground as I charged towards him, yet the distance between us was still too great. "FELIX!" I screamed.

Logan was behind me, the rustling of the long grass sounding like a hundred snakes as we raced to his rescue. I tried to run. I screamed his name once more when I got to the lake's edge, unable to see any sign of him.

Without a moment's hesitation, I dove in; the sudden rush of water filled my ears and the icy-coldness of the water bit into my flesh. It was dark, murky as I tried to see him, my arms flailing in front of me, desperate to find him. *No, no, no.*

The waves crashed against my body as Logan dived into the lake. His movements had kicked up silt from the lake's bed, causing more shadows to obscure my vision.

My lungs were on fire, holding my breath as I continued to search, occasionally breaching the surface to get another lungful of air before diving straight back down. I could hear the distinct squawking of the raven nearby, sounding like hysterical laughter. *Torvus didn't show me this.* I thought as I sliced through the water, getting closer to the centre center lake. *Perhaps something has already changed?*

Logan was shouting above the surface. The water muffled and distorted his voice, but I could faintly make out my name. *"Have you found him?"* I asked in our telepathic connection; unable to hide my hope.

"No, have you?"

"No."

I dove lower to the bottom of the lake. My hands sifted along the muddy bed, feeling strange, solid objects beneath my fingers. At first I thought they were just rocks, except one had holes in it and another was strangely long and thin. Pulling them up to my face, I found they were not rocks at all. *Bones.*

I choked, gulping in lungfuls of water in panic. Reaching up for the surface, kicking away from the bottom of the lake with every ounce of energy I have left. The harder I kicked, the more it felt like hands dragging me back into its depths.

When my face finally broke through the surface, coughs racked my body, spluttering uncontrollably as I swallowed mouthfuls of water. My eyes scanned every direction looking for Logan. *"Cass... I have him."*

Several feet behind me Logan re-emerged from the lake, our son draped over his arms. Sodden and dripping as he carried him to the long grass. His skin was pale and cold to the touch, his eyes closed as if he were sleeping.

"Is he breathing?" I asked, but Logan's somber expression was not the answer I had wanted. "Let me try... I can..."

Logan dropped to his knees and started to perform chest compressions. He didn't speak, blocking his thoughts from mine as I knelt beside him sobbing. "Logan... let me try."

Logan refused. "This... isn't... something... you... can... heal... it's... not... like... a... few... scratches..." He said, his words matching the staccato rhythm while tears rolled down his cheeks. They hit me like a slap to the face, but now was not the time to be hurt. I needed to focus, to concentrate.

Placing my hands on either side of Logan's. I thought about the water in his lungs, imagining it rising up his windpipe and spurting from his mouth. *I will not let him die.*

"Perhaps this would be a kinder death," a male voice echoed in my mind. I flinched, twisting my head to see who it belonged to. *"You know Jax has something much worse planned for him."*

"Torvus?" I asked, turning to face him, eyes scouring the landscape, "Torvus, please help..." I cried, "*Please!*" My voice cracked as I begged, feeling my energy ebbing. Logan refused to cease in his efforts to bring Felix to life.

A black bird appeared out of nowhere; much smaller than the one that attacked us. It transformed before my eyes into a black mass that took the form of a human. Colors gradually bled through the darkness; subtle and vague hues, like a vintage photograph. By the time he reached me, he looked just as he did back in Mount Hejha; every line and battle scar etched into his face. The tattoo of his allegiance was prominent against his pale skin.

Torvus dragged his fingertip over Felix's forehead, brushing the limp, wet hair out of his face before placing his palm flat against his bare, damp skin. In an instant Felix's eyes snapped open, and he began spluttering and retching water. I watched as Felix's skin changed from pale to its usual pink.

Logan scooped Felix into his arms. Tears of happiness and relief spilled down his cheeks as he looked at me, silently inviting me to join them. Wrapping my arms around both of them we all sobbed.

"Was that the same shifter that attacked us? The raven?" I sobbed.

Through small slits, Torvus watched us; his mouth pulled in a straight line, the muscles in his jaw set. He slowly nodded. "All his children are shifters; all of them are *ravens.*"

"Who's children?" Logan asked, his attention piqued, his anger obvious.

"The Phantom's."

"Who are they?" I asked. "Do we know any of them?"

"There are many, too many, his seed sown throughout the land and time. They could be anyone."

Silence cloaked us like the finality of death. Even Felix, wild-eyed and dripping wet, remained utterly still. It was Logan's thoughts that were shouting. Screaming in frustration as he reeled off names; suspects of who this person could be, but Torvus merely shook his head.

"It is always someone you least expect," Torvus warned, his eyes hardening. He stared at the three of us, his body transforming before our very eyes back into his form of a crow. *"Enjoy your time together, for I fear it will not last for long."*

THIRTY

Jax

Alyiah was lying in wait for me, consumed by her impatience and lust, as I knew she would be; her legs splayed wide on the bed with her eyes closed. Soft moans escaped from her parted lips as she drove her fingers deep inside her slick entrance. It was perfect. She was too distracted to detect my return, too oblivious to know what was yet to come.

I licked my lips, my instinctual and carnal desire taking the reins on my body as I inhaled the scent of her sex. I was going to stoke the fire that burned within her, to torture the truth from her. *There is nothing wrong with enjoying myself while I do it.*

The compulsion to bury my face between her thighs overtook me, despite the rage emblazoned through every fiber of my being. An animalistic growl emanated from my chest; as the door slammed shut behind me. The sudden bang startled her, but before she had a chance to move, I was already upon her.

My hands pushed her thighs wider and my mouth curled against her dripping folds. I felt her body quiver under my touch. She cried out as my tongue plundered her, leaving her breathless. While her hands reached out for me, clutching fistfuls of my hair to hold my head still. Alyiah's hips bucked against my mouth, frantic and desperate.

"Jax!" She cried. "Oh, fuck..." Her orgasm ripped through her body. Her muscles spasmed while I alternated between thrusting my tongue deep inside her pussy, and sucking hard on her clit to make her scream.

I pulled my face away from her slit.

Her juices clung to my lips and trickled into my beard; I frowned; I hated the beard, the consequences of living life on the run. Alyiah preferred this more rugged look; she was turned on by the danger of this lifestyle–and the monster I had become appealed to her darkness.

Her hands pawed at my recently inked skin. Black thorny vines trailed up my arms and spread across my chest. They continued to stretch across my back and finished up strangling me at the base of my jaw. The tattoos were a status symbol; a pledge to the pirates - I could withstand pain. I could commit. They were a demonstration of my endurance. I was one of them now - an outlaw.

Alyiah's eyes flitted over my skin, lingering at the bulge in my pants. "Why did you leave me like that?" she whimpered; her hands gravitating towards it. A groan instinctively left my lips as her fingertips danced over the strained fabric. It throbbed, demanding its release.

"What riled you up before?" She asked, her voice husky. "Didn't those other women make you cum like I do?" she purred, "but, you know, if you want to free my darkness, the easiest way is to feed me blood."

It was as if a switch had flipped inside me. My lust converted back to anger once more, but I was cautious about showing it. *Not yet.* I reached for the rope at the end of the bed, forcing a playful smile onto my face.

"I thought we could make things more *fun*." Alyiah's eyes widened, her body tensing, but reluctantly she nodded. Alyiah knew better than to disobey me; never would she have the nerve to refuse my commands.

Smirking with anticipation, I could sense the hunger sizzling inside her. Once a dormant volcano, now active and ready to erupt. The thought of her being bound thrilled me. Knowing Alyiah would be vulnerable and completely submissive filled me with exhilarating power. I wanted her to be afraid. *I thrive on power and undeniable fear.*

Once I tie her limbs to the bedposts, she will not have the ability to transform. *She will have no escape.*

This offcut of rope, abandoned at the port in Lythenall, was too short for mooring a ship, but *perfect* for tying up a human. I had stowed it in my duffel bag, not really sure what I would use it for, but knowing that it would come in handy one day.

Back then, the duffel bag had been practically empty. Stolen from a nearby village, all it contained were sneakers and clothes. Over the course of the few years on the run, my men and I had scavenged what necessities we could. *Where there was a will, there was a way.* I found I could fuck my way through the town, paying lonely, unsatisfied wives some attention. They were only too eager to offer food and clothes, and even money, on the back of a promise of a return visit. *I never did.*

These days, the duffel bag was full, splitting at the seams with cash and gold bars, as well as rare and valuable artifacts. All items I had pilfered during the raids with the pirates used to extend my support. Used to buy more men and weapons, to pay for repairs to ships in preparation. *My time to claim the throne is coming. Logan and his guards will never know until it is too late.*

I recalled the last raid; three villages plundered. Their temples were full of golden statues, with gems embedded in intricate designs. Silver plates and candlestick holders. Brass prayer book holders and footrests. Most were too heavy and cumbersome to carry, but I grabbed whatever I could carry and shoved them in my duffel bag. It was a heavy burden to lug around from place to place. I had to keep it safe. I paid the landlady a hefty sum of money for the use of a lockable chest. It was bolted to the floor of an innocent-looking broom closet beneath the stairs. I even paid her extra for her to ask no questions and hand over keys that could unlock it; wanting to be the only person who could access my treasures while we were docked here.

I wrapped the rope around my wrist, ignoring the searing pain in my shoulder, the ache in my back, the unrelenting pain in the palms of my hands. All injuries suffered during raids to prove myself to the pirates; putting myself in harm's way to save another, just to guarantee my cut of the loot.

When I had retrieved the rope, the landlady had startled me; her tinted-blue permed hair bobbed up and down like a jelly on top of her head in the shadow she cast over me. The potent floral perfume she wore clogged my throat and made my head spin. I was not sure how long she had been standing behind me, perhaps only a few seconds, but she had seen far too much.

I spun around, catching her off guard. She had no time to scream, to even register what was happening when I thrust the dagger into the side of her neck. Blood gurgled in her throat as a river of crimson spilled from her mouth. Forceful sprays erupted from her wound as I yanked the blade away from her, her body falling towards my outstretched hands. I watched in morbid fascination as the color drained instantaneously from her skin and the light behind her eyes faded.

There was a triumph that filled me, a gratifying feeling, as I watched her life ebb away before me. Though I did not have time to linger, nor to dispose of her body - not while Aliyah was waiting for me upstairs. I unceremoniously shoved her into the broom closet;

breaking the shelves full of cleaning supplies as her body fell against it. Eventually she landed beside the mop buckets, arms and legs splayed in unnatural angles. *You shouldn't have been such a nosy bitch*, I thought as I snatched up my duffel bag from the trunk and locked the closet door.

It did not take me long to secure Alyiah's hands and feet in the rope. Fastening them with the strongest knot known to any sailor. Her resolve had ebbed away; like putty in my hands. She was willing to give herself over to me completely. Yet she could not hide her fear as it intensified with each tight knot. I loomed over her, staring coldly down at her. *Weak, defenseless. Nothing.*

My knees spread her legs as wide as the rope would allow as I shoved my thick, solid cock deep inside her. She squirmed at the sheer force of it, her eyes bulging, and a small whimper escaped her. My palm slammed down on the side of her face, pushing her face into the bed. A red mark bloomed underneath my hand.

"Keep quiet, bitch." I hissed, moving my hand down to her throat. Applying just enough pressure to restrict her intake of breath without causing too much alarm. Alyiah's eyes flickered up at me, glassy with fresh tears.

"Jax... you're hurting... me" Her voice came as nothing but a croak. I ignored her, tightening my grip around her throat. Smirking as the tears fell and rivers of mascara stained her cheeks.

"I know what you fucking did." *Thrust.* "I know you fucking betrayed me, Alyiah." *Shove.* "What I don't know is why." *Choke.* "Why, Alyiah?" *Thrust.* "Why did you betray me?" *Pound.* "What the fuck did you say to *her?*"

There was no restraining my brute force as I took her. The headboard crashed against the wall; the knocking of wood on stone reverberated loudly, though it did little to drown out her pitiful whimpers.

My heart hammered inside my chest, pumping my blood around my body in a rush as my hatred took control. Shoving a wad of bedding into her mouth, stifling her cries as I lifted her ass off of the bed. I ran my tip between the crack of her buttocks. Slamming hard into her rosebud entrance with no warning. She squealed loudly, thrashing at the ropes that bound her feet, leaving red marks on her skin.

"I know you were behind her disappearance." I hissed, the sound of her ass cheeks slapping my thighs filled the room. I pulled on a fistful of her hair, yanking her head backwards. I watched as she struggled against me.

"Did you really think I would not find out?"

Every muscle in her body tensed. Her ass clenched around my cock as if that was going to stop me. If anything, it increased my pleasure as I continued to fuck her tight ass relentlessly. *Her pain, my thrill.*

Anger and jealousy crept over me; Cassidy's joyous reunion. Hundreds of miles away, at this exact moment, my brother fucked my soulmate - in *my* castle, in *my* kingdom.

I roared as my grip tightened in her hair; sinking my cock deeper and harder into her. I was close, *too* close. I relinquished my hold on her, pulling back and letting her body crumple to the bed. Her ass gaped and her body heaved with ragged breaths.

"Why did you do it?" I asked, kneeling beside her. Her hair wrapped between my fingers, yanking on her neck as hard as I could without snapping her neck. "Why would you betray *me?* After everything I have done for you?"

My hands trembled as adrenaline pumped through my veins. I forced my fingers into her mouth, yanking it open, preparing it for my member. I could not stand the sight of her. The more I stared into the eyes of the woman who undermined my efforts to reclaim my throne, the more I wanted to kill her.

I spat in her face, stroking my rigid cock over her cheeks and smeared her nectar over her lips. Voluntary or not, she was still wet. I no longer cared who her father was. I wanted to belittle her, to shame her, taking my sweet time humiliating her. *No one gets away with trying to betray me.*

"Jax..." she pleaded, her words muffled by my fingers. "I didn't... I never-" I tore my fingers out of her mouth, part of me wanting to hear her pathetic excuse. "I haven't seen Cassidy... I haven't left here... I would have been with you... if you weren't *busy elsewhere.*"

My hands pinched her cheeks together, my patience waning.

"But... Cassidy... she doesn't..." Alyiah tried to stifle her sobs. "She will *never* love you... not like I do."

My hand found her throat. *How dare she talk about Cassidy as if she knows her, as if she understands how she feels. She loves me. If she didn't, I would be dead now.*

The veins beneath the thorny vines inked on my arms bulged. I squeezed, watching the blood vessels burst in her eyes. Seeing the color in her face change from a bright right to a violent shade of purple. My thumb pressed down hard on her larynx; rendering her incapable of talking or breathing. Her eyes were drooping shut as she lost consciousness.

"Look at me... LOOK AT ME!" I roared, feeling Alyiah's pulse grow weaker beneath my fingertips. My other hand pumped my shaft frantically, overcome with the need to release my load along with my pent up anger. Her eyelids fluttered open, glassy and distant as her life slipped away.

I watched as the light in her eyes dimmed. "I was never going to make you my Queen," I sneered. Enjoying the sadness creeping into her eyes, savoring her defeat as she stopped trying to fight back.

Alyiah had accepted her fate. One last act of submission to me as she drew her last breath. It pushed me over the edge.

My orgasm erupted violently, causing my toes to curl and every muscle in my body to spasm as I came. My load spurted in rapid waves over her face. Coating her forehead and cheeks in thick white globules before smearing the last few drops over her blue-tinted lips. *She does not wear my cum as good as Cassidy.*

Flashbacks of Cassidy on her knees in her tiny bedroom in Fic danced in my mind. Recalling Cassidy's elegance and beauty as my essence trickled down her face. Remembering the way her tongue licked at the corners of her lips and her eyes burned with the desire to taste it. *No one ever will. Cassidy is one in a million. She. Is. Mine.*

When Cassidy is beside me in her rightful spot, it would absolve all my darkness. Every evil deed would be worth the blemish upon my soul. Cassidy will forgive me. I had no doubts about that. *But can I forgive her so easily?*

I need to see that she regrets making the wrong choices. *I need to feel her genuine remorse for her actions.* After all, she may be my soulmate, the woman who I wanted more than anything, but without me, she was nothing. *Perhaps I need to make her a bit more aware of that.*

Killing Alyiah had always been part of my plan, though *not yet,* and not *like this.* My anger and distrust in her had pushed me too far. Now, I had a body with no means to dispose of, and no explanation to give her father. *He will not take kindly to the murder of his protégé.*

I cursed under my breath as I removed the ropes from her wrists and ankles. They had made deep gouges in her flesh, and purple bruises bloomed around them. In parts, the cuts had bled, and the friction burns showed the extent of her struggle against them. There was no way in Hell he could find her *this* way; no way he could know I am to blame for his daughter's demise. *What the fuck am I going to do?*

The room was spinning along with the frantic thoughts in my head. My eyes fixed on her lifeless body; her head lolling to one side like a broken doll. *Fuck.*

There was still too much that needed to be done: the pirates, the witches, those *babies*. If The Phantom knows I am behind him, every intricate thread of my tapestry of revenge will unravel.

I turned my back to Alyiah, slamming one fist onto the wooden desk. I had worked hard to get this far and fail; too much time and effort had been spent, so much blood has been spilled in my mission to take back what was mine. *I have gone too far. There is no going back.*

With a loud growl, I swept everything that was on the table to the floor: a map, some balled up parchment paper, a hairbrush. For a moment. I had forgotten about the lit candle. I watched as it rolled away from the desk, catching the dry sheets of paper alight.

Laughter flowed out of me like a river bursting its banks. Uncontrollable waves, sinister and unpredictable. This was it - the solution to this problem. *Fire.*

I watched as the flames danced across the map, sparking an idea in my mind. A crazy, ill-thought out method of how I could dispose of not just Alyiah's body, but of that of the landlady's too. Reaching over the flames I grabbed the candle. The flames reached up from the map, grazing the flesh on my forearm as myu fingers wrapped about the wax base of the candle. My eyes darted around the room as my plan hatched in my mind.

The sorry excuse for drapes that hung around the narrow window, the bedding beneath Alyiah's lifeless corpse, even the old thread-bare rug beneath my feet were flammable; holding the candle against each one until the fabrics ignited. I growled in exasperation as the flames slowly crept across the different materials, each one proving just how insignificant this plan would be without some kind of accelerant. *I need something else. A fuel of some kind that would truly obliterate everything.*

It was like a lightbulb moment, as my eyes stared at the flickering flames; recalling the boiler the landlady's head smashed against, the old thing looked a little *faulty.*

Without a backwards glance I left the room, fumbling around in my pockets for the keys, my fingers clutching at nothing. *Shit, where did I put it?* Pausing momentarily I placed the candle on the reception desk and patted down my breast pocket; relief washed over me as the sharp points of the keys dug into my fingertips.

I unlocked the closet door once more; stepping over the mangled, bloodied corpse until I could reach the boiler, now dented and splattered with its owner's blood. I scrutinized the access panel, tearing at it until it came away revealing the crucial piece to my plan: the input valve. *If I could cause a slow leak, my insane plan might just work.* I fumbled with the valve, twisting and turning it in every direction trying to loosen it, beads of sweat spotted my forehead as the thing refused to budge. *Fuck.*

I had almost given up hope as I continued teasing it one way and another when suddenly it snapped off in my hand and a rush of foul-smelling gas hit me in the face. *shit... that's too much.*

The gas hissed as it escaped at an alarming rate; my mind trying to calculate how long I would have to escape when my duffel bag caught the candle, flinging it off the reception desk and towards the closet.

Not fucking long enough.

I dived out of the entrance, clutching my bag tightly to my chest, rolling on the ground and staying low as I heard the explosion.

Smoke clogged in my throat as the windows shattered, raining shards down upon me; the intense heat clawed at my back as the inn erupted into flames. I crawled across the debris that had been thrown out of the building from the blast, as onlookers gasped and screamed in horror.

They ferried around me, fussing over my superficial wounds, crying out for help. Over their shoulders I could see the inferno I had started had become uncontrollable, like Hellfire, consuming everything in its path. It had one sole purpose—to destroy. *Just like me.*

Nothing was safe from its scorching grip. Everything was going up in smoke, including my perfectly orchestrated plans. *Nothing is ever perfect.*

Slowly I rose to my feet, guided by their helping hands, while the chaos reigned inside the building across the street. The crackle of the blaze as it reached up to the night's sky, catching the thatched roof ablaze. "I think... my girlfriend... she was inside..." I choked, allowing the tears caused from the stinging heat to fall from my face.

They all spun around, their faces a picture of horror as the flames reflected in their eyes; giving them enough of a distraction for me to slip away unnoticed. I was a traumatized victim, fleeing the scene, I would act my way out of suspicion should it come to it.

With one final glance over my shoulder, I smirked. *Perhaps the Gods are on my side after all.*

THIRTY ONE

Cassidy

I tossed and turned all night, unable to wake from this dream; flames blocking every exit like a wall of fire closing in around me. The heat caused sweat to bead on my forehead, drenching my clothes until they stuck to me like a second skin. Smoke burned my lungs as I inhaled their toxicity. Yet I could not move; could not take my eyes off of the creature on the bed. Its majestic wings spread wide; its neck poised at an unnatural angle.

I knew I should feel sorry for its tragic death, but I could feel nothing but hatred towards the creature. Instantly recognizing it as one of The Phantom's children—a raven. Blinking back the sweat that trickled along my brow, I noticed that the figure on the bed was no longer that of the black-feathered bird. Instead, it took on the form of a woman. Naked, but still very much dead and broken. Someone I knew *very* well. *Alyiah.*

Gasping for air, my throat sore and hoarse, I awoke, finding Logan's compassionate eyes staring at me. Our son was crying in his arms.

"Cass...you were screaming," he said. "You woke Felix, and no doubt half the castle."

I sat bolt upright. *Is Alyiah the one who attacked us at the lake?* I thought. My heart was hammering against my ribcage.

Logan frowned. "I mean, it's possible, but Jax was last seen twelve hours ago." He paused, rocking Felix in his arms in a vain attempt to soothe him. "He was seen in Halen *with* Alyiah." Despite myself, I felt my jealousy stir; the soulmate felt like a noose around my neck. It strangled all sense of rationale from my thoughts. "It would take around three days to get here-"

"On land!" I interjected, slouching back into the duvet, cold shivers crashing through my body.

Logan's brow furrowed as he tuned into my train of thought. But *how long would it take a bird? Flying across the open oceans completely unobstructed?*

We stayed in silence, only the sound of our heavy breaths filled the room. Felix had finally fallen back to sleep.

"I'm going to put him in his room," Logan whispered, looking at the temporary crib erected in our room. I had wanted to keep him close following his near-drowning incident. "Flynn owes us some babysitting duties," he added, disappearing out of the room before I could object.

My eyelids were heavy, drooping closed, but my mind refused to switch off while panic and fear thundered through my body. The room seemed to close in on me, the ticking of the clock marking every second I spent alone here. I could not relax, with my mind replaying the visions on a continuous loop. Felix's lifeless body, Logan's dismembered head, and now Alyiah's charred corpse. *Alyiah*, the broken raven.

Among these visions, I tried to work out where Alyiah fit into Jax's plan; *What would she achieve by attacking us? Was she acting for her own gain? Or carrying out her father's demands?* In truth, Jax didn't want the kingdom, not really. Sure, he wanted power and control to dominate and command, but he enjoyed the freedom much more. The ability to travel without responsibilities. *He has no intention of making her Queen.*

I jumped out of my skin the moment the door opened once more, unsure exactly how long Logan had been gone; realizing that the only reason Alyiah would have attacked me would have been to separate us. By coaxing Felix into the river, trying to maim me, it would have left us vulnerable. *Had Jax told her about the bond? That it would break if one of us died? Was she trying to kill me like Demi before her?*

"Cass..." Logan hushed, his metallic hand scraping back the covers; his lips seeking mine as he climbed into the bed beside me. My natural instincts took over, allowing his warm embrace to envelop me. I was consumed by my need for him: his closeness, his love, and the sense of safety.

His kisses traveled across my cheek, along my jaw, and down my neck; a brush of cold against my nipple in contrast to my warm body as his hands slid beneath my nightdress. They cupped my breasts, while his hot mouth worked its way up to them; gently biting them, making me gasp out loud as I savored the sensations.

I held his head in place, thrusting my breasts closer to his face, silently inviting him to keep going. Logan's tongue traveled down my stomach that was scored with stretch marks. I pushed his head lower. Clamping it tightly between my thighs as soon as his tongue flicked over my sensitive nub.

Clutching his dark hair in my hands, I felt myself finally let go of my apprehension. Though they were temporary, those moments of bliss as Logan's tongue lapped at my clit were like heaven. Spreading my legs wider, Logan slid his metal digits inside me.

"They are curved for the ultimate reach of that sweet spot of yours," He whispered with a smirk, finding that spot that made me moan instantly. My body buckled, writhing uncontrollably; becoming wetter with each stroke. Feeling my inner thighs becoming slicker and my nectar dribbled out of my tight slit. *I am so close already.*

With a determined grin, Logan quickened his pace and increased the pressure he was putting on that sweet spot; my body's natural reaction to grind against him. Again and again until I came, and when I did, my climax was breathtaking.

"Do you want me now, my Queen?" Logan asked, bringing his face back up to mine, smelling the sweet scent of my juices on his breath.

I drew his face closer, allowing my tongue to part as his lips coated in my nectar, savoring the taste.

"I will always want you." I smiled, feeling his solid shaft slide against my soaking wet mound, teasing my entrance open. "I will *always* choose you."

In one swift thrust of his hips, my entrance welcomed his full length. Both of us moaned in unison. My body was designed for him, to bring us both the maximum amount of pleasure. Slow and steady, we matched each other's rhythm. Our actions were in perfect synchronization; we had become one entity amidst our pleasure. I felt our bond tighten around us, our hearts close and our bodies even closer as they pressed against each other. Our soft pants quickened as our climax neared, but we were in no hurry. Neither of us wanted this moment of our absolute union to end.

"I love you, Cassidy," Logan whispered. "Those words don't seem enough... there are no words that will truly describe how much you mean to me." His words danced over my lips, our beating hearts hammering as ones. "Since the moment I first saw you at the lake, until my very last breath, my heart will always belong to you."

The bed was cold. Logan's side was empty. The usual sounds of the morning; the hustle and bustle of the castle reverberated off the stone walls. For a moment, I almost allowed myself to believe that things were normal, *happy*; that I had just woken up from the most bizarre and terrifying dream. I almost believed that none of it was real; that Felix had not nearly drowned and there was no threat of Jax's vengeance looming on the horizon. But the pang in my chest and the worry in my heart told me the truth - *trouble was coming.*

Though I had not expected it to come so soon, there was a sudden clatter of metal upon metal; the sound I instantly recognized as the clashing of swords. The screams of fright pierced through the halls, a macabre harmony with the cries of the wounded. But it was the deathly quiet that followed shortly after that echoed the loudest. The silence of the slain.

I could hear them all, but worse, I could *see* them too, which could only mean one thing - my worst fear had come true. *Jax was here, inside the castle.*

I looked on in horror, my body paralyzed, as the blade cut through the air effortlessly. It sliced through flesh and muscle as it chopped its way through the throngs of guards trying to defend the castle. *Trying to defend us.*

The sword bearer raised the blade above his head; taking a deep breath before bringing it down through the slightest gap in the guard's armor between his neck and collarbone. A fatal wound; the sword sunk to the hilt, shattering the guard's ribcage as it descended. Cracking any remaining bones as the sword bearer yanked it back out again.

I could taste the bitterness of blood in my mouth. The stench of death cloyed my nostrils, and I felt the triumphant glee inflate my chest as the guard toppled forwards, his armor hitting the ground with such force the metal buckled. It may have only been a minor victory, but as my host looked around at the other guards' lifeless bodies littering the floor - it was one of many.

Most of the guards were not in full suits of armor, having shoved on whatever items they could in a hurry. They had been caught off-guard. *I warned Logan that Jax would always do the unexpected.*

The once rustic and original beige stone floors were now ruined. Blood of the wounded trickled in the gaps, staining them a deep scarlet. The tapestries that had hung on the walls for centuries, now torn and covered in blood spray. The halls were slowly filling with Jax's soldiers. No matter how hard our guards fought, there were suddenly more of them, these *undead* soldiers; resurrecting our slain men to join Jax's cause.

My host's eyes scanned his army; a sense of sick pride coursed through his body. Every single one of Jax's soldiers was decomposing before his eyes. I watched as the closest soldier stumbled along with skin hanging off his graying bones. White tufts of wiry hair hung on the scalp that was slowly sliding off its skull. Another swung a rusty cutlass toward a guard, its innards spilling from its rotten gut and pooled at its part-flesh, part-skeletal feet.

"How are you liking the show?" Jax chuckled. *"Don't worry, the best part is yet to come."*

I stifled my scream. Pushing myself out of his consciousness, but he kept me hostage. *"I want you to have front row seats to this, Cassidy. I want you to see it and feel it. The moment you become mine... and mine only."*

Jax's speech was interrupted, his trail of thought abandoned.

"Argh, Jax, what is the plan now?"

My breath caught in my throat as my host looked over its shoulder in annoyance. Quickly glimpsing his reflection in the cracked mirror in the entrance hall. Gone was the boy I remembered, well-groomed and full of charm. In his place stood a burly man, stubble stretched across his chin.

Black tattoos wrapped around his muscular arms, broad shoulders and thick neck. His hair was now long and pulled back into a braid. Black soot and dust covered his rugged, handsome face. The biggest difference was his eyes.

Vivid blue saucers, full of malicious intentions, stared back from the reflection. I felt their scolding heat as they burned into my soul. I felt a pang in my chest; gone were the wild, jovial eyes I admired. Gone was the boyish charm and handsome smirk that drew me to him at the Masquerade of Whispers. My chest contracted as the sobs wracked my chest. I wanted to scream and cry, to mourn him. The Jax I knew, the Jax I loved, was gone, as if he had died on the battlefield.

"Jax... is that really you?" I whimpered.

I felt him shrug his shoulders, ignoring my words.

"I may have changed just a little bit since we last saw one another," Jax's internal voice said, his eyes still glaring at his reflection. His focused stare kept me rooted inside his mind. *"Do you like what you see?"*

Shaking my head, I tried to make him look away. *"Look at me, Cass... Look at what I am... because of you,"* he sneered, *"You believed exile was a kinder fate than death... what do you think now? What do you see? A Monster?"*

I bit my lip, unable to answer him. *"Years of torment, ridicule... wanting everything that Logan has, because you chose him over me... Well, now you have front-row seats to watch as I take it all back."*

He spun around to look at those who flanked him. *"Do you remember them?"*

A band of scantily clad witches stood before him. Balls of colored flames emanated from their palms. I felt Jax eye them up greedily as his mind replayed parts of their rendezvous.

"I am not all evil," Jax added while recounting the moment he sliced the throat of their master. *"I freed them. I gave them their powers back... perhaps I will keep them after all this is over. Would you like that?"* The desire that oozed in his thoughts made my cheeks grow hot, profusely blushing at my arousal.

I suppressed a sigh; *"No, Jax, I do not want that. I want my family. I want Logan."*

Jax's anger simmered beneath his skin as he walked beyond the witches. Each footstep was loud and heavy, like his heart. A dirty and disheveled pirate came into his line of sight. He donned a leather trench coat over his muscular frame. The material barely stretched over his bulging biceps. A flash of a red bandanna wrapped around his forehead; his face looked older than his years - hard-worn and scar-pocked. A battered and faded black tricorn hat sat upon his head; a large singular black-iridescent feather protruded from the tattered red ribbon that wrapped around the center.

"Let's get this over with." A harsh voice reverberated in Jax's mind, causing him to look to his right. A huge, ominous figure, cloaked in darkness, hovered in mid-air. The white, expressionless mask was facing my host, dripping in fresh blood splatter.

I gasped. The mask was similar to the one Jax had worn at the Masquerade of Whispers all those years ago. Except it was not Jax's piercing blue eyes staring out from beneath it, only an endless black void. The brilliant white mask was a stark contrast to the black abyss that was the Phantom.

My host flinched. Wiping his thoughts suddenly, trying not to alert this being before him of my presence. Jax nodded, lifting his arm so I could see it. The sword's blade was slick with red, dripping the blood of his slaughtered victims. Innocent lives lost in the castle. I shuddered. *"You knew I was coming for you."* His voice reverberated in my mind. *"You know nothing or no one will stop me... You are mine..."*

I tried to pull out of his mind, but he held me in; a prisoner to witness the atrocities he was yet to carry out. *"Everything I have done, and will do, is for you... for us."*

Jax cleared his throat, glancing from side to side at his mismatched band of allies. His words made the hairs on the back of my neck stand on end and a shiver ripple down my spine.

"It is time to reign in Hell. Let the blood flow. We will paint the walls with their guts... so I can seek my revenge."

THIRTY TWO

Jax

I am a monster; born from hatred and jealousy, leaving nothing but death and destruction in my path. No longer held by my morality. Driven purely by my own selfish desires. The throne, the Kingdom. *Her.*

Cassidy.

My soulmate. *My* lover. *My* World.

Everything I have done, everything I have achieved, all the lives I have sacrificed was for her. For *this* very moment.

The time is now to seek my revenge. I will show them I am a King that commands respect.

Slowly I began to remember small snippets of time where the monster inside had taken control. The sword ripped through flesh like scissors cutting through paper. Severing arteries and ripping through tendons as if they were nothing but string. Sprays of blood coated me from head to foot; not a single patch of my clothing was not saturated in crimson.

As I looked around the room, I could not tell you whose life force I took first; father or son, but I knew one thing was certain - *I won.*

Yet, it did little to calm the chaos that seized control over me. The monster was still there; lurking beneath the surface - too angry, too riled up to tame as I stood in the room, taking in the bloodied mess. Snippets of the massacre coming back to me: my hand tearing into the young boy's chest. The warmth of his heart was like a hot stone in my hand. It had throbbed a few last beats in my palm before it fell still forever.

The father, my brother *Logan,* was outraged; I had never seen him react in pure rage and hatred before. He had always been one to steer in the face of caution, his words from our sparring sessions echoed in my head. *"Don't act in anger. Rash and foolish decisions could be lethal."* His own words of wisdom had been lost on him as he launched himself at me with nothing but the fire of his fury and determination in his eyes.

He refused to allow the tears that blinded him fall as he raised a metal spear that was in place of where his hand should have been. This new attachment to his false limb made his movements bulky. *Predictable.* He had always been the better fighter, more agile and quick-witted in the heat of the moment. If I had not taken his sword wielding hand in the war, he would have stood a better chance.

For the first time in the entirety of our lives; Logan had fought with his emotions unchecked; letting his heart guide his sword. *"Fighting with your emotions is how you find yourself dead."*

It had made him weak, *vulnerable;* his rage claimed as he swiped at me erratically, leaving himself open for my fatal blow. My sword pierced his heart, the shock flooded his eyes as he dropped to his knees. Incoherent words lingered on my brothers lips as he stared defiantly up at me; catching only a snippet of his last words: *"Cassidy will never forgive you."*

The monster within emerged once more in a blur of unadulterated rage; growls resonated from my chest as my fingers dug into his flesh, twisting and tearing with inhuman strength as I tore his head from his body. The Phantom had not lied when he placed an enchantment on me; *I am unstoppable.*

The satisfying pop as his skull was separated from his spine, the wet, squelching sounds as sinews of muscle and flesh tore. My heart thumped in my ears and a smile crept across my face the moment his body dropped to the floor with a sickening thud, leaving his head still clutched in my palms. I brought it up to my face, talking to him as if we were having a civilised conversation. "Perhaps you should have taken your own advice." I smirked. "I guess you were right about that after all."

My eyes fanned around at the once white walls. Each one dripping with fresh blood. It was beautiful; *it was art.* A canvas painted for everyone to see, demonstrating the lengths I had gone to and how far into insanity I had sunk in my mission to claim all that was mine.

Dizzy and disorientated, the monster I had unleashed had taken its toll on my body. *It is not easy tearing a human limb from limb.* It had left me breathless, my muscles sore and my body exhausted. I still needed to get to her. *My real prize. My most valued possession. The one thing I wanted more than anything else in Xeyiera.*

I forced my feet, one in front of the other, to stalk the corridor that spanned from the prince's room to their room. The blood on my clothes left a trail in my wake. *Drip, drip, drip.*

The castle was silent now; the persistent dripping from the trophies in my hands was all that I could hear. *Drip, drip, drip.*

Each drop echoed louder than the last. A staccato beat, like a metronome. The rapid whooshing of the adrenaline in my veins was the crescendo. The soft padding of my feet as I drew closer to her room was the drum roll to the finale. *The encore.*

I felt the warm blood trickle between the gaps in my fingers. The splatter of each drop hit the beige stone floor. My trophies from her dearly beloved was all the proof I needed to show her I had won. *The only two people left that stood in my way.*

I had warned them. *All* of them.

Things never had to be this way; Cassidy had a choice, but she made the *wrong* one. Perhaps her sympathy and guilt for Logan had been mistaken for love. Yet, she could not let me die, preferring to have me exiled. *Was she secretly hoping that I would come back for her one day?*

All those years ago, I did not mince my words. *Nor did I break my promise.* The heart of her child was in one hand, the head of my brother in the other. Logan should have been more careful. Cassidy should have made the right choice.

I could blame her until I was blue in the face, but deep down, I knew it was *my* weakness that had been my ultimate downfall. The deep-rooted love for my brother, my sentimentality, had rendered me incapable of killing him on the battlefield all those years ago, but it was done now. The war is over and the bond that linked the three of us was destroyed.

I am the victor. I am King. Cassidy belongs to me.

As I drew closer to her door, I chuckled to myself. *Did Cassidy really think I would accept defeat?* Gone were the days when life would serve me everything on a silver platter; if I wanted something I had to take it. *Who would have thought a prince would prefer a pirate's life?*

I felt no rage or remorse as she stood there, though perhaps I should have.

Cassidy is here. *She is mine.*

Her eyes were wide with shock, with horror. Her screams were loud enough to wake the dead; *if The Phantom had not reanimated them already.* I could see her hatred towards me, her eyes reflecting the evil atrocities that I had committed; that she had witnessed first-hand.

I am a monster. This is what I have had to become to reclaim what is rightfully mine.

We were the two remaining soulmates; our fate forever sealed with my brother's blood. I knew it would take time to ease her pain but our bond will help her heal. She will love me. *Cassidy is mine.*

I longed to embrace her, to soothe the pain I had caused, to show her that all of this was necessary so that we could finally be together - just me and her. I missed the tenderness of her hugs, the feeling of her warm skin against mine; inhaling that familiar fragrance, I have not smelled for years.

I had expected our bond to have felt stronger now that Logan was gone. *Forever.*

Cassidy was no longer screaming. Instead her hand was clamped over her mouth, wide-eyed in horror as she looked upon the face of her husband. A deathly silence fell over us, so quiet that the only sound I could hear was the blood dripping on the floor beneath my feet. I stared at her as she stood frozen in place, biting her trembling lower lip and refusing to avert her gaze from her massacred husband's head.

My heart thumped wildly against my ribcage, adrenaline still pumping through my veins, but the glow of victory had quickly dispersed. With bated breath, I waited for her reaction; but only stony silence welcomed me.

"Not exactly the warm welcome I'd hoped for," I muttered, barging past her as my eyes took in every detail of their room, disliking the way Logan's belongings were mixed with hers. Seeing his shoes and his clothes through the open closet door, all sitting beside hers. His nightstand held a glass that had a slight smudge of lipstick on the rim. The thought of him sharing the same glass, touching her, *being* with her repulsed me.

My gaze fell on the bed, the bedsheets ruffled, the slight indent on the mattress where their bodies laid beside each other night after night. *He should never have been here, it should have been me.*

Logan's head fell from my hands, landing with a loud, solid thump. The heart of her only child still clenched in my fist. *I had warned them. I had told them what would happen.*

The green-eyed monster embraced me once more. A growl erupted from my chest as I spun on my heel, picking up his head once more. Swinging it around, using it as a battering ram to destroy everything within reach. Everything that was on the vanity desk fell with a crash to the floor; scattering in all directions.

I glared at the head of my brother as his soulless eyes stared back at me, casting his silent judgement over me—over what I had become. I could still feel the tearing of his flesh beneath my fingertips as I ripped at the last sinews. Removing his neck with my bare hands, as I had seen Alyiah do to Nate.

This was my trophy of triumph; undeniable proof to one and all that I was *the new King of Eyre.*

I stared back at him, a smile stretching across my lips. *I told you, brother, I will have it all.*

I spun on my heel to face her. I wanted to seal our soulmate bond while the blood of my brother was still wet on my hands and blade. I was going to plant a seed of my own inside her; to replace the child I had taken from her.

But as my gaze settled onto the space where she had once been, I realised she was gone.

THIRTY THREE

Cassidy

I felt it snap, like an elastic band stretched too far until it inevitably broke. The *scissa amor vinculum* bond was no more. The soulmate bond that held the three of us in a chokehold was now destroyed, taking my heart along with it.

Logan and Felix are gone.

The thought of never seeing them again was too hard to accept, but there was no denial of the gaping void that swallowed me whole. My heart, as brittle as glass, shattered into a million pieces.

My nails carved deep moon-shape crescents into my palm. The small vial was tightly clutched in my grip as I backed out of the room. Jax was too absorbed in his own thoughts I could no longer hear.

I glanced at the stopper of the vial poking out from my clenched fist. It was a miracle that any of them had survived Logan's wrath. Yet this one had rolled seamlessly to a stop at my feet, as if Fate was guiding it to me.

With each sickening thud of Logan's head against the wooden desk, I felt my stomach heave. Logan did not deserve this treatment; neither of them deserved their barbaric and untimely ends.

The walls were closing in around me, the air thick and heavy, suffocating me. I had to leave - *while I still can.* Taking each step quietly, my eyes trained on Jax's every movement.

From deep within my soul, I was numb. I tried to process everything I had watched; to accept that I would never see my husband or child in this life. I could not even bring myself to feel regret knowing that three years ago I could have prevented all of this.

My fingers tightened on the only unbroken glass bottle of *Instant Death*. I took my chance the moment Jax's back was to me. My bare feet pounded against the stone floor. My heart raced as fear and adrenaline became the driving force of my every movement.

My ears strained as I listened for Jax; knowing it was only a matter of time before he noticed I had gone - *before he came after me.* For so long I could channel his thoughts, see through his eyes, feel his presence to gauge his proximity to me. Now there was a complete disconnect; nothing. It was jarring; but I also welcomed it.

"Thank you, my son-"

I froze, peering over the banister. A hushed conversation floated up from the entrance hall below. *"You have done well... all things considered."*

A glimpse of floppy blond hair; the broad shoulders and a stance I recognized from any distance. *Flynn.* The Phantom's hand was placed on his shoulder while letting out a low chuckle. *"You shall remain here undetected. No one, not even yourself, will ever know the truth. You will forget your involvement, forget that you are my son..."*

It was easy to slip into Flynn's mind; for decades we had communicated this way. His thoughts were like my own. We had used it to pass our tests; to get ourselves out of trouble, but I wasn't prepared for this revelation. We were all led to believe Flynn was Elder Jeremiah's son, and it was clear in Flynn's thoughts he nor Elder Jeremiah knew any differently.

I gasped loudly, not realizing that I had been slowly creeping down the stairs. The white mask whipped around to face me as I froze on the last step. The Phantom's two black soulless eyes bore into my soul.

"Seize her." His voice reverberated in the empty corridors; at first I wondered who he was talking to. When suddenly, armored forms rose from the floor; the undead soldiers reanimated once more; all of them facing me.

Jax's animalistic growls erupted behind me, startling me back into action; prompting my feet to take a different path - one I hoped would lead me to safety. The thunderous sounds of Jax's footsteps were quickly gaining on me, bellowing my name at the top of his voice while the footfall of soldiers followed him.

I had been so caught up in my thoughts that I had stopped concentrating on keeping my balance, the blood-slick soles of my feet made each step treacherous. My foot suddenly slid out from beneath me as I crashed into a ceramic vase on a plinth. It shattered as it fell to the floor.

Scrambling to my feet I recalled Logan telling me about the history of the vase; created by the first humans to walk Xeyiera. It was a crude design, and the colors had faded with the passing of centuries. It was one of the most valuable pieces on display in the entire castle. *Logan would be mortified if he found out,* I thought just before a sharp pain sliced through my chest. *Logan will never know. He is dead.*

Something metallic caught my eye as I cleared the last of the shards. A black gemstone shimmered under the castle's light. The stone was held captive in an intricately twisted metal cage with a sliver of a silver chain attached to it. I found myself staring at it, captivated by it.

"CASSIDY" Jax roared as he stood at the end of the corridor. Without knowing why, I snatched it up before continuing to escape the castle. "CASSIDY!" Jax's anger was palpable. A sinister, threatening tone crept into his voice. "You can run, but you can't hide. We will always belong together. You cannot deny our bond."

I held my breath as I entered the kitchen; the aroma of simmering soups and roasting meat still lingered in the air. It would have smelt delicious under different circumstances, now it just made my stomach heave. Especially as my eyes darted around at the scene, bloody handprints smeared across walls. Blood drops mixed with the white flour-dough of the fresh bread that had been abandoned on one worktop, and fresh vegetables half-chopped on the other. The chefs sprawled on the floor, a debris of food, pans and shattered plates surrounded them; their once brilliant white chef overalls now stained with crimson.

I stifled a sob, tiptoeing over the dead bodies as I made my way to the other side of the kitchen. My sight firmly fixed on the door to the courtyard - my only chance of escape. *If I can just get there before Jax gets to me-*

There was a crash behind me as the kitchen doors sprung open. *Too late.* Jax roared as he threw himself over the kitchen island. His fingers wrapped around my neck as he pinned me to the wall, Logan's head was still clutched tightly in his other hand. I choked back tears as he thrust the severed head in my face.

"Tell me Cass, why didn't you let the Elders hunt me down and kill me after the war if you didn't want me?"

He let Logan's head drop to the floor, my eyes followed it as it landed unceremoniously at my feet. Stepping back he let his grasp around my neck go, the anger in his eyes softened to hurt. "Cass... I love you... "

I no longer felt numb. I felt anger, hatred. *Disgust.* I saw the silver of silver out of the corner of my eye: The hilt of a chef's knife. I grabbed it and slashed wildly in Jax's direction.

Jax let out a surprised yelp, staggering several feet away from me, giving me my last chance of escape. I bolted; slamming the door behind me, too scared to look back at what I had done.

I ran through the courtyard, trying to ignore the sight in my peripheral vision. The corpses of Logan's guards resurrecting from where they had been struck down, taken by surprise. Their limbs splayed in unnatural positions, bones jutted out of their bodies; their mortal wounds still wet. Slowly they were beginning to flank me on all sides. *They will be upon me before I reach the gate.*

The wooden door behind me burst open, I could hear Jax's pained groans as he tried to follow me. *How badly had I hurt him? Was it enough?*

The gravel crunched beneath my bare feet, tearing them to shreds as I staggered towards the gate; noticing traces of blood left behind after each step. I winced in agony; my lungs were on fire as I forced myself not to give into exhaustion. Yet it seemed the more steps I took, the more the grounds stretched on endlessly as my aching body grew tired.

A flash of black ripped through my vision; the flutter of black wings before my eyes. *Torvus! Take me away from here.* I begged. *Please.*

My hands reached out to him, forgetting momentarily about the vial. It fell in slow motion, shattering as it hit the ground. Shards of glass glittered like stars while the contents seeped through the gravel, turning the moss and lichen brown and dry.

Footsteps were fast approaching, not only Jax's but those of two others. I glanced over my shoulder, to see Flynn and The Phantom approach. I stood there, defeated; willing to accept my fate. *What is the point of running?*

They were almost before me when the crow's outstretched wings blocked my vision. Its talons digging deep into the flesh of my shoulders as Torvus' voice whispered softly in my mind. *"Close your eyes, Cassidy."*

When I opened my eyes, I half expected to be back in the mountainous terrain of Mount Hejha. *Not here... anywhere but here.*

For a moment the lake seemed so peaceful, as it had always been, until I noticed the wild flowers withering before my eyes. Their petals falling to the ground, shedding them like tears of mourning. This had always been *our* place; *our sacred spot.* Being here without Logan felt wrong.

The crow was perched at the lake's edge, pruning its feathers with its black beak.

"Why did you bring me here?" I whimpered, my sobs building in my chest, threatening to burst at any moment.

"Because this is your favorite place-"

Out of nowhere, a raven swooped down. Its talons pierced the crow's chest, its malice and conviction clear in the way it hissed. A scream involuntarily escaped my throat as the raven flew off with the crow in its grasp.

"Flynn... is that you?" I asked, watching as the raven faltered, the crow slipping from its talons. It hovered in the air, both of us watching as the crow fell to the lake, causing a small splash as it sank to the watery depths.

"Flynn... this isn't you... You must find a way to defy him... your father... your real father... I love you Flynn, you were always like a brother I never had."

The raven hovered for a few more seconds. Its black, beady eyes seemed to search for something. I thought I saw a glimmer of recognition flash in its eyes before it cawed loudly and disappeared into the darkening sky. Leaving me all alone.

Alone. Forever alone.

I watched the surface of the lake, praying for Torvus to resurface. Deep down, I knew he never would. The way his bird-like body fell, limp and bloodied, he was gone before he touched the water. A sudden realization hit me; there was only one other person who knew the existence of this lake. The one who had interrupted Logan and I, the day we had first met. *Flynn is the raven who attacked me, not Alyiah.*

Time no longer seemed relevant. It stretched endlessly as I sat at the lake's edge, succumbing to the shadows where the moon's silver glow could not reach. Branches of the weeping willow draped into the water, but no longer did it bear any leaves. In fact, the longer I sat here, the more this oasis of natural beauty seemed to suffer.

Under the blanket of night, everything was monochrome. The once fragrant wild blooms wilted. The sunflowers Felix had been so fond of hours before were now drooped over and shriveled; their petals spilling onto the long grassy floor, reminiscent of the pools of blood I had witnessed in the castle.

My favorite flora, tulips, were now bathed in darkness; their vibrant reds and yellows dulled to complete black. Only the stark white lilies seemed to thrive, the aroma filling my lungs as I inhaled a long, deep breath. I had no more tears left within me. I was empty, numb, left alone to face the reality of life without either of them.

This was the place we had first met all those years ago. The place that had changed my life. I felt as soulless as one of the resurrected corpses under Jax's command.

I am no longer afraid of dying, but of living without them.

It was not only my heart that shattered the moment Logan took his last breath, our rare bond had been too fragmented. *As scissa amor vinculum*, the broken love bond, a curse that had led to the destruction of all happiness and hope.

Jeremiah failed to inform us that when one of us perished, the bond would break completely. *That* was why it was important for me to decide—to choose the prince my heart truly desired. He knew it would only be love, *true love*, that would survive. The love that Logan and I had - it was real. I thought we would be together, living out the end of our days in the castle.

I would give up my dreams of traveling. I would happily be a caged bird as long as I was with Logan and Felix.

The more I thought about the breaking of our bond, the more I struggled to comprehend whether Jax had felt it shatter, too. *Or was he too absorbed by his need for vengeance?*

It was possible that he was so blinded by rage, hate, and ambition that he had not noticed. But I had noticed, even as I writhed on the bed, sharing the agony of Logan's last moments. Not only seeing the attack, but *feeling* Logan being butchered by his own brother. Until the fatal blow came, when Jax's blade had struck his neck. Then I felt nothing.

The moment he stood before me, nothing more than a heinous villain, I knew I could never move on.

I will never be safe. Not in a world where this monster exists.

The water was cool against my flesh. The watery depths gripped my nightdress like unseen hands pulling me into their watery depths. The sludge and slurry of the lake's shore squelched between my toes, as I allowed those hands to guide me.

I knew that I, like Torvus before me, would never emerge.

As I ventured up to my neck deep, I paused, not out of hesitancy, but to look up at the sky. Noticing only two stars glittering brilliantly against the black velvety sky. I knew it was them, Logan and Felix, their souls ready to embrace me once more.

Take me to the place where I belong. Take me to them. Take me home.

EPILOGUE

Jeremiah

Her dress floated elegantly on the surface. Her hand resting over the black onyx necklace at the base of her throat. A small smile forever frozen on her peaceful face.

At first glance, she looked as though she had fallen asleep, floating on the surface of the serene lake. Basking in the iridescent glow of the moonlight while gazing up at the starry night sky. But I knew it in these old bones of mine-Cassidy would never wake.

Gone, just like that. A flame that had once burned so fiercely, so easily snuffed out. Leaving nothing behind, only memories and dreams of what could have been. The love they had shared was pure and true. The Kingdom would have thrived under their leadership. They would have left behind a formidable legacy. *Had it not been cut so tragically short.*

I recalled the only love I ever had; the biggest regret that burdened my soul–Agatha. She, too, had met a similar end; following my command to walk into this lake, never to resurface. Often I thought of her, her watery grave beneath. Wondering whether she wandered the lake until the soul inside her perished. *How long had it taken?* Not dead, yet not alive; stuck somewhere between the two. Suffering because of my command, she had no choice other than to obey. I preferred to think she had drowned instantly. I sincerely hoped she had slipped back into eternal peace where she belonged.

Sometimes I thought I saw her face peering back up at me beyond my reflection: eyes full of sorrow, hands reaching out to pull me under to join her. My darkest secret tormenting me from her watery grave. Bringing her back was my biggest regret that will never fade with the passing of time. *Time does not heal. It is the excuse used to make humans feel better about allowing themselves to forget.*

There was a reason this lake never appeared on any maps, becoming Xeyiera's best kept secret. Only those who stumbled upon it in person ever knew of its existence. Cassidy had been the first human in over three decades to discover it.

I wanted to preserve the beauty of this place. To let nature absolve the evil that lurked within the murky depths of the lake. This lake was not called The Lake of Lost Souls without a good cause. Although the serene surface looked tranquil, beneath it was nothing but a watery grave. Hiding the darkest, bloodiest part of Xeyiera's history, as well as hiding my own selfish past. My brother Zeke used this place to dump the bodies of those he sacrificed, as well as those he could not resurrect.

Although Zeke was banished, Xeyiera will never be free of him. After all, he was still one of us, an Elder. Immortal and inhuman. No matter how hard I tried to live like them, I would never feel the glorious embrace of the afterlife.

The sun was rising as Cassidy's body began its descent into the murky waters. The orange haze banished the shadows and blinded me. The glare bounced off the gentle ripples, obscuring my vision. Although I could not see it, the lost souls that lurked in the depths welcomed Cassidy with open arms. *Agatha, my beloved, please take her with you to the afterlife.*

If only Cassidy had listened to Elder Quinn, their lives would have been so very different - longer, happier, and filled with love. He rarely spoke, but when he did, those who listened would have done well to heed the warning in his wise words. *"One day you will regret not sinking that dagger into his neck when you had the chance."*

In her last moments, did Cassidy regret her decision? I wondered. Her corpse disappeared from view; sinking to the bottom of the lake, taking with her the ancient talisman: Bronwyn's necklace. The first witch. Zeke's wife. The White Raven.

It was Bronwyn's parting words that resonated with me. *"Nothing lasts forever, only the sweet release of death."*

ABOUT THE AUTHOR

Raven has been weaving narratives that traverse a myriad of genres and topics since childhood. Through her journey as a writer, Raven has honed a distinctive voice that resonates with readers, spinning tales of adventure, romance, mystery, or of fantastical realms and ethereal entities. In each intricately crafted page of her books, she embarks on journeys to places afar with lovable and relatable characters, inviting readers to escape from the reality and monotony of everyday life.

As a wife and a mother of two, life can be chaotic, yet Raven still dedicates as much of her free time as possible to bring to life ideas from her vivid imagination, in the hopes her readers find her stories transformative, inspiring and entertaining, with the aspiration to share this gift with audiences far and wide.

When she is not outside tolerating the unseasonable British weather, you will find Raven as a consistent online presence on most social media platforms, where she offers regular updates and new insights for upcoming releases. She is always happy to chat with her readers and followers.

Find Raven's other books or leave a review on Amazon or Goodreads

Website: https://www.ravenleitheharlow.co.uk/
Facebook: Raven Leithe Harlow – Author
Instagram: @ravenleitheharlow.author
Twitter/ X: @RavenLeithe

SCAN ME

Printed in Dunstable, United Kingdom